Praise for *I Am Lucky Bird* by Fleur Philips

"…one of the most stunning and visceral books I've read on child abuse this last decade. It is so brilliantly and beautifully written I found myself holding my breath through many of the passages…I highly recommend *I Am Lucky Bird* to all of my readers. 5 stars.

—The Bookish Dame Reviews

"Philips' writing flows off the pages…The story still haunts me in many ways and the images that filled my head while reading are not easy to forget…I think Fleur Philips needs to be applauded as an author for adding special moments of beauty to such a tragic story…This novel deserves nothing less than 5 stars."

—Roxanne Kade

"…it just blew my mind; how an author can even write about the various themes incorporated into this story is honestly beyond me. This read was absolutely amazing. Reread list? Definitely going on it at the very least. It's a story I could never get sick of."

—Violet Journal

"I read this book in one sitting, it is just so powerful…Although the subject matter is dark, the story is rich and powerful. A must read book, with spectacular writing and a protagonist who has found a special place in my heart."

—Minding Spot

"Philips portrays a completely genuine character living a life that, unfortunately, is completely plausible and realistic…A truly lasting and emotional story, *I Am Lucky Bird* is a novel that has carved a home in my heart. Highly recommended."

—Jenn's Bookshelves

"Fleur Philips is an excellent writer. *I Am Lucky Bird* is a beautifully written debut, even while the subject matter is difficult to read…Very Highly Recommended."

—She Treads Softly

"This is a gripping story, and you won't be able to put the book down."

"A story that will capture the hearts and minds of readers."

"I finished this book in one, less than 2 hour sitting—I couldn't stop reading it. Period...It's hard to believe this is the author's debut novel!...Lucky's tale will stay with you, and make you want to share the book with everyone you know!"

"I can literally say I do not remember the last time I felt so connected to a character. I feel very strongly about this book, as I think it is an excellent tool for teaching. I think that schools and book clubs for teens everywhere should consider this book for utilization. There are some marvelous lessons to be taught in here, and great discussion points. I would not tell an adult book club to turn this one away either, as it is truly a book worth talking about. I can personally say that I am looking forward to whatever may be next in Fleur Philips' writing career."

"...a deeply emotional book that would stay with me for hours after I put it down and for days after I read the last page...Hands down, one of my favorite reads of 2012!!"

"Beautifully written, raw and dark in places, haunting and ethereal in others, *I Am Lucky Bird* will seduce the reader, capturing Lucky's emotions perfectly, allowing them to share her horrors, her downfalls, her despair, as well as her healing, her rebirth and her success, as if she were a part of our family. This book will settle under the skin, and live there, and deliver a tale of strength and deliverance that is unique and beautiful, from page one, to it's final word."

"This is just a non stop book, beautifully written. I am highly recommending it!"

—A Novel Review

"Beautifully written and featuring a young girl with a strong voice, author Fleur Philips tackles sensitive subjects such as child abuse, abandonment and coming of age with quiet strength."

—Reader Girls Blog

"It's simply a spectacular book…I can't wait to see what Fleur writes next!"

—Lauren's Crammed Bookshelf

CRUMBLE

Fleur Philips

Copyright © 2012 by Fleur Philips
ISBN: 978-0-9889299-0-6

Text composition by Clark Kenyon
www.camppope.com

For Gayle

"Darkness cannot drive out darkness: only light can do that. Hate cannot drive out hate: only love can do that."

—Martin Luther King Jr.

~ 1 ~

A sudden flutter in my stomach wakes me up on Monday morning before my 6 o'clock alarm. It starts low, but then creeps upward into my throat, causing a cool sweat to break across my brow. I shudder as I sit up, the glowing numbers from my alarm clock next to my bed casting neon green across the room. It's dark except for that kryptonite glow and the streaks of early dawn pushing through the blinds covering my window.

I hear the voices of birds outside, and I want to hold my breath and just listen to them for a few seconds, but the nausea makes me forget they're even there. Pale light filters through the crack beneath my door—Dad is up and in the kitchen downstairs. He's the early riser between the two of us, never sleeping past 5:30, even on the weekends. I smell the bitterness of our morning coffee.

Is it stronger than normal, or is it just me?

"Oh, God."

I cover my mouth with one cold hand and yank the covers away from my body with the other. My Victoria's Secret PINK pajama bottoms stick to my damp thighs as I run across the beige carpeted floor. I try not to make too much noise as I hurry to the bathroom across the hall and fall onto my knees in front of the toilet. I heave a few times, my stomach clenching into a knot, and when the spasms settle, I lean back against the porcelain bathtub and wipe at my damp eyes.

"That was lovely, Sarah."

The nausea lingers, but I stand up and wash my hands, then splash cold water on my face. I stare at my pale reflection in the mirror, my chin-length and normally straight blonde hair ratty and twisted from sleep. Other than my eyes appearing dull like aging moss in comparison to their normal vibrant green, I think I look okay. I take a deep breath and wait, watching as my cheeks slowly blossom back into their natural peachy hue. I brush my teeth and take a shower, then finish getting ready for school before going downstairs.

"Hey there, sunshine," Dad says.

He's sitting at our small round dining room table, sipping coffee and reading the newspaper. Current technology hasn't swayed him from keeping to a tradition. I cross the living room, setting my school bag on the sofa, and walk into the kitchen.

"You feeling okay?" he asks.

From the corner of my eye, I see him looking at me. I turn and smile, "Yeah. Why?"

He takes a sip from his coffee mug, then looks back down at the newspaper in front of him, probably the financial section by now. "I thought I heard you throwing up earlier. That's all."

The top of his freshly shaved head is still shiny from his morning application of skin tonic. He was in his late 20s when he'd finally given up hope of ever having a full head of hair. He'd been shaving his head ever since. He's a big man, 6'4" and thick. When I was little, he had more muscle than fat, but with each passing year, his belly more and more slips over the edge of his jeans. I don't mind his expanding waistline, though. He's always been like a big teddy bear to me. The excess weight just makes him more snuggly.

"No, Daddy. I wasn't drinking last night."

He smiles. "Well, why the heck not?"

He tells everyone I don't drink because I'm smarter and more mature than most of my classmates, and maybe I am, just a little (I've had straight A's my whole life), but that's not the real reason. The first time I went to a house party and drank was the last time, and Dad knows it. I was in 9th grade. It was after a football game. I'd tasted beer a few times—a sip here and there from Dad's Pabst Blue Ribbons. I didn't like the taste of it, but everybody at that party was drinking, and my best friend, Megan Cochran, and I didn't want to look like wimpy freshmen, even though we were. We ended up doing beer bongs, and I threw up for three days. That was it. I haven't touched a drop of alcohol since.

I take a coffee mug from the cabinet and set it on the counter—feeling mildly less hung over than I did in 9th grade, despite drinking nothing but a Coke last night—and pull the coffee pot from the machine. The black liquid swirls around and around inside, and I swallow against the rising vomit in my throat as I put the coffee pot back in its place, the warmer sizzling as though pissed I didn't take my morning's share. On any other day, I would've. I love my coffee, the sweetness of the vanilla creamer and my one single scoop of sugar—not the artificial kind Dad uses, but the real stuff. Pure. White. Refined. But the sight of the coffee this morning—not to mention the pitchy odor of it—makes me want to puke again.

I take the loaf of sourdough bread from the refrigerator and cut a piece of it in half, then drop the two slices into the toaster before sitting at the table.

"You sure you didn't have a few wine coolers or something last night?" Dad asks. "Definitely not like you to skip your coffee."

I push the thought of sipping on a wine cooler from my head as I pull the community section from the newspaper and stare at the headline—*Time Again for the Kalispell High School Spring Fair!*

"I promise, Daddy." I don't meet his eyes. "Alcohol was not a part of my study session with Megan last night."

Would've been tough, considering I wasn't with Megan last night.

"Alrighty, then," he replies. He rises from the table with his coffee cup and empty plate and walks into the kitchen. "Want me to put butter on your toast?"

If I didn't tell him not to make breakfast for me, he would. He only stopped cooking me eggs and bacon and toast every morning when I turned 16, but only because I asked him to. I was too old to not be taking care of my own breakfast. If he had his choice, he'd baby me for the rest of my life.

"You're the best, Daddy."

He winks and smiles, then pulls a slice of toast from the toaster and tosses it back and forth between his fingers before dropping it on a plate. Watching him reminds me of a game we used to play— a soccer skill—when I was little. The ball was a "hot potato," and the point of the game was to keep the soccer ball from hitting the ground by continuously bouncing it on our feet. We'd count how many times we kicked the ball without it dropping, and whoever had the highest amount of kicks, won. It took a few years of practicing the skill before I finally beat him. To this day, though, I think he let me win, just so I'd work harder every time thereafter.

He walks into the dining room and hands me the plate of toast.

"Thanks, Daddy," I say. I pick up the section of newspaper he'd been reading. "Anything worth looking at today?"

"More people out of work, housing market continues to tank. Plenty to read, sunshine, just not good news."

"It'll get better," I say.

"Not with you-know-who still in office."

It's not President Obama's fault, Dad.

I didn't like Barack Obama at first either, but not because of what he was or wasn't doing for the country. I didn't actually follow the man's campaign. Why would I have? I was 15 years old when he was elected. All I cared about then were my friends and boys, weekend parties, playing soccer in the fall and skiing in the winter. I didn't like President Obama back then because Dad didn't like him. And wasn't that normal? I don't know many kids at my school whose political views aren't shaped by their parents. Dad has his reasons for not liking the president. For one, Obama's supposedly a threat to gun owners, and Dad owns a gun shop. But that isn't his main reason.

"Eat up, sunshine," Dad says. "We'll roll in ten minutes."

He walks through the living room and up the stairs. I take a small bite from a corner of a slice of toast, but it becomes thick and sticky in my mouth, and I gag as I swallow it. I drop the remaining toast into the garbage can, cover the wasted food with a paper towel—because I *hate* wasting food and somehow covering it makes me feel less guilty—then walk into the living room and grab my cell phone from my school bag. There are three text messages—one from Megan and two from David.

Hope you and David actually studied last night. ☺

Megan's been my best friend since the end of 5th grade when she moved to Montana from Minnesota. During recess one day, I watched her dribble a soccer ball between her knees, the mess of curly black hair on her head bobbing up and down. I knew how to dribble a soccer ball like that, but she was better. When I asked her if she could show me, she tucked the ball under her arm and looked up at me—she's a foot shorter than I am—and smiled. We've been soccer teammates and skiing partners ever since, and there's really nothing that can come between us. Girls are girls, though, and we've had our "moments," but we always seem to find a way to work through them. I have other girlfriends—mostly my soccer teammates and a few of the other ski bunnies—but over the years, each of them showed her ugliness in one way or another. Whether it was talking behind my back and then denying it to my face, or pretending not to be interested in a boy I liked, only to sneak off into the woods with him at a party when I wasn't looking. I think the fact I didn't drink made it easier for them. They'd used the "I was drunk" excuse, and I had to give them some slack.

But for the past two years, the girlfriends I walked away from were the ones who pretended to be just fine with me being friends with the three black boys at our school, but then mocked it in front of anyone else who questioned it. There were a few rumors that spread about David and me after we started seeing each other, but we denied it, and because we've been keeping our relationship a secret for over nine months, it's tough to argue our denials.

Miss you already.

And I love you.

"You ready, sunshine?" Dad says from the upstairs landing.

I slip my cell phone into the front pocket of my school bag and zip it shut. "Yep."

"You kids and your text messaging," he says as he descends the staircase.

"Megan's quizzing me on our economics exam," I say. I lift the shoulder strap of my bag over my head. I hate that I have to keep lying to Dad. Before David, I never hid anything from him.

"Well, then, maybe text messaging does serve a purpose."

I follow Dad out the front door and to his old blue Chevy truck parked in the driveway. On the ride to school, I watch our neighborhood pass by. It's one of Kalispell's oldest—small, square, two-story homes with wrap-around porches and cookie cutter A-frame roofs. I've never lived anywhere else. Neighbors have come and gone, and with the newer ones came changes. Some of the houses have new paint or prettier yards, or there's been a garage added or a bedroom or a bathroom, but our house hasn't changed a bit. For all I know, it looks the same as when Dad bought it after we moved to Montana from Alabama when I was just a few months old.

Dad pulls into the drop-off zone in front of the high school and stops the truck behind a Volkswagen unloading the Marshall twins.

"You'd think with all the money they have, they'd make them boys cut their hair," he says.

Tim and Jonah Marshall are freshmen at Kalispell High—bleached blonde snowboarders with Southern California, laid-back surfer attitudes. They moved to Kalispell from San Diego the year before after their parents decided snowboarding was safer for the boys than surfing. On a Saturday bus trip to Big Mountain last December—the ski resort 20 miles north of Kalispell where I learned how to ski and where Megan and I spend every Saturday from opening day to the start of soccer season—I overhead the boys say David was "the shit."

"He's the next Jerry Rice," they'd said.

They were sitting in the seat in front of Megan and me. I don't know the boys that well, but they were talking loud enough for me to hear. I think they wanted me to know they approved.

"Have a good day, Daddy," I say as I slide out of the truck.

"Need a ride home after school?"

"Megan'll drop me off."

"You can use the truck tomorrow, sunshine," he says, "if you want. I won't be needing it during the day."

I smile. "That's okay. Megan can take me home."

I love Dad more than anything in the whole wide world. He's the only family I have, and I know there's not a single father on the planet who's more amazing than him. But no matter how wonderful he is, there's a part of him I don't understand, and I'm not sure I ever will. Two years ago, I didn't notice it so much. I didn't care about the Confederate flag bumper sticker on the back of his truck. But at a spring track meet that year, Megan walked up to Jalen Parker and Reggie Powell and introduced herself. I remember trying to grab her arm to stop her. I didn't have a reason, other than I thought I wasn't supposed to like the boys, and when they reached out to shake my hand, my body trembled, but I don't really know why. If Megan and I had never become friends with them, and eventually David, I might've been just fine driving Dad's truck. Not caring. Not knowing.

The bumper sticker makes some people laugh—people who know Dad and like him. I'm pretty sure they think it's an old sticker left there by the person who owned the truck before us, but I know better. It makes other people angry, just as his gun shop does. But those people don't speak up much. It's only obvious because of an occasional grumph or curse, too quiet for anybody to really hear. And to another group of people altogether, the bumper sticker is praised. Those are the people David and I need to keep our relationship from, and as much as the other groups make up the people we see everyday—parents of classmates, teachers, coaches—so does this group. Joe Berger's father is in this group. Last fall, he deliberately tried to get David kicked off the football team, saying David had given his son a black eye following a practice, but everybody knows it was Randy Cooper who punched Joe in the face after he called David a nigger.

Randy was the first of my classmates to become friends with Reggie and Jalen. He'd actually volunteered to show them around the school on their first day, and he's kept by their side ever since. And when David moved to town, Randy was thrilled to find out he played football. Randy lost a handful of friends because of Reggie, Jalen and David, including Joe Berger. Randy and Joe were inseparable in elementary school, but Joe had no interest in hanging out with "blacks," and Randy had no interest in remaining friends with a racist. After Randy punched Joe in the face, David asked him why a skinny white cowboy would give a shit about a black outsider.

"'Cause my daddy didn't raise me that way," Randy had replied. "He taught me that everybody deserves to be respected. We're all God's children, no matter what the color of our skin. You ain't done nothing to Joe to deserve his bullshit. And you been nothing but a friend to me."

Randy told Reggie and Jalen the same thing when they asked him why he volunteered to show them around. They both thought it was some kind of joke, and Randy's response had been, "Why you judging me based on my hat and boots? I ain't judging you."

But Joe Berger and Joe Berger Sr. aren't the ones I worry about. Their intolerance is obvious.

"Hey Mr. McKnight!"

I recognize the voice behind me. It's Alex Mackey.

"Hey Alex," Dad replies. "I'll see you at 4 o'clock, right?"

"Yep!"

I keep my eyes on Dad. He wrinkles his forehead and makes a twirling motion with his finger, indicating he wants me to turn around. I roll my eyes, but I follow his gesture anyway. Dad can't stand it when people are rude.

"Hi Alex," I say.

He smiles at me. He's thin and pale, his buzzed black hair making his ears, eyes and nose appear bigger than they really are. Both of his cheeks are pock-marked with acne scars.

"Hey, Sarah. How's it going?" he asks.

"Good." I try to keep eye contact with him, but his silence makes me nervous, so I look down at my feet.

17

"Okay. So, bye," Alex says. He takes a few steps back before turning around and walking away.

"You could be a little nicer to him," Dad says.

I turn back to the truck and place my fingers on the window ledge. "I know, Dad."

"Things ain't real easy for him," he says.

Everybody knows Alex's home life is a mess. His father's drunk more than he's sober, and his idea of a fun Friday night is putting his wife in the hospital. According to rumors, Mary Mackey always had an excuse. One time, she apparently told the ER doctor she fell down a flight of stairs. When the doctor expressed his surprise she hadn't broken an arm or leg, Mary said she was carrying a load of laundry. The clothes must've provided a cushion.

"And you're rescuing him, right?" I ask.

"Well, somebody should. I'm just giving him a place to feel safe, Sarah. And he's earning some extra cash while doing it."

Alex had been working at the gun shop for two years—stocking supplies, keeping the place clean, running errands. Dad even put a cot in the back room so he could sleep there if and when he needed to. The only reason why Alex hadn't yet been invited to the house is because he's had a crush on me since the 5th grade, and it makes me uncomfortable. We were friends back then, the way lots of kids are before they get older and wonder why, and by the time I turned 13, I didn't want to be Alex's friend anymore. I wasn't trying to be mean to him. It just…happened. But Alex has never stopped paying attention to me, and he's made it more obvious this school year than ever before. He's always looking at me, and when I catch him staring, he turns his head real fast. He reminds me of a peeping tom, or worse, a rapist checking out his next victim. I'm not afraid of him, though. He's harmless, but he nevertheless gives me the creeps.

"I had somebody in my life who helped me," Dad says. "And if it hadn't been for him—"

"I know, Daddy. You might not be here at all."

I didn't know my grandfather, but from the little Dad's told me, he wasn't much different than Chuck Mackey—drunk, abusive, mean. He died when Dad was 18 years old. By then, Dad had already left and was living with the man he said saved his life—a man named Clive Sanders. But that's all I know about him. His name.

"Alex is a nice boy, sunshine."

"I know, I know." I step away from the truck. "Love you."

Dad waves and drives away.

I hear the familiar tone of my cell phone telling me I have a new text message. I pull it from the front pocket of my school bag. It's from David.

Meet me at our spot?

I type back, **Be there in a minute.**

David's and my "spot" is an empty space the size of a large closet beneath the south staircase, just outside of the senior hallway. The south doors open to the staircase, and unless you're a senior, you wouldn't walk into the adjoining hallway. At the end of that hallway is the senior cafeteria. All of the classrooms are upstairs.

All of our friends—those who think it's cool we're a couple—stand as a shield in front of our hiding spot so we can, every once in awhile, have the chance to act like every other couple in the school. It wasn't our idea. Reggie and Jalen came up with it, and the rest of the group agreed. I thought it might get old for them after awhile, but nobody's ever complained. Truth is, I never thought I'd have to be jealous of the girls who can openly hold their boyfriend's hand or make-out with them in the corner of the cafeteria at lunch, but I am. Beyond our secret spot, David and I are just friends. I know there's other kids at school who probably don't care we're a couple, but they don't publicly show they're okay with it. I'm not mad at them, though. In high school, reputation is everything. And for the most part, Reggie, Jalen and David aren't treated any differently than anybody else, as long the mingling of blacks and whites stays within the boundaries of friendship. But for me to be dating one of them?

By the time I make it to the south entrance, the senior hallway is full, and Megan, Randy, Emma Morgan—another soccer teammate who moved to Kalispell from Seattle at the beginning of the school year—Reggie, Jalen and David are all gathered next to the staircase.

I glance at my watch. Five minutes before the first bell.

I see David move behind the group and under the stairs, so I greet everybody and knock knuckles with Randy and Jalen. I can't get away from Reggie without a hug, so I wrap my arms around his neck and squeeze. He smells like Old Spice, musky and sweet—always just a bit too much, but he wouldn't be Reggie without it.

"It's my love potion," he always says.

When I finally sneak behind the group and below the staircase, I press my lips to David's. His hands are on my cheeks as he kisses me, his tongue warm. Familiar butterflies erupt inside my stomach, and as we continue kissing, the flutter moves down and below my belly button where it settles. I want to be alone with him, somewhere, wrapped in his arms, the warmth of his body pressed to mine. But when the tingling doesn't fade from my stomach, I pull back from him, the queasiness of nausea overwhelming.

"Baby, what's wrong?" David asks.

I take a deep breath. "I don't know. I feel…sick."

He laughs. "Gee, thanks. Don't think I've ever done *that* before."

My skin is clammy and warm. I feel light-headed.

"Sarah?"

I place my hand on David's cheek. His eyes are the color of cinnamon, a good two shades lighter than his skin. Reggie and Jalen both have eyes like black coffee, so when I first met David, I couldn't stop staring at him.

"Don't be a jerk," I say.

Reggie shouts, "Heads up!"

That's our cue we need to come out, which always means me leaving first and moving behind the boys until I'm up next to the girls who are standing the furthest away from the hiding spot. David follows 10 to 15 seconds later and cuts sharply left so he's at the opposite end from me.

Reggie's warning this time isn't really a warning at all. The bell is about to ring.

"You gonna be okay?" David asks.

I nod, but I'm not really sure. I kiss him one more time before stepping out behind Reggie and Jalen. Megan and Emma walk with me to my locker so I can drop off my bag and grab my calculus book. At the sound of the first bell, we hurry back down the hall and up the stairs.

"See you guys at the break," Emma says as she ducks into Mr. Grey's economics class.

Megan and I share first period calculus with Jalen. The three of us drop into our seats just as the second bell rings. I open my book and stare at the black scratches of lines and numbers and graphs, the mess of ink swirling oddly across the page.

What the hell?

I lift my eyes to Mrs. Keatley. She's writing on the chalkboard, her kinky brown hair pulled into a puffy ball on the back of her head. It looks like a round of yarn freshly attacked by a thick-clawed cat. As I'm watching the blob of ratty hair, the wave of nausea strikes again, stronger than before and deep enough to cause my body to shiver. My skin is damp with sweat.

Oh, no.

I jump from my desk and run out of the classroom and toward the open door leading to the staircase. On the landing is a garbage can. I know it's there. When I round the corner, I lean over the edge of it just in time to throw up into the trash bag.

~2~

Alex Mackey is sitting at a desk in the front of Mr. Grey's economics class when he sees Sarah McKnight run past the open doorway, one hand covering her mouth, the other holding her stomach. When he hears the sound of her vomiting, he looks at Mr. Grey.

"That's just gross," a girl says from the back of the room.

As the vomiting continues, a chorus of whispers and groans rises.

"Now, now," Mr. Grey says. "Open your text book to page 52 and start reading. I'll be right back."

He leaves the classroom, shutting the door behind him, and as soon as he does, the chorus of voices grows louder. Nobody's going to read anything on page 52 when someone's puking in a garbage can on the other side of the door.

When Mr. Grey returns, the voices stop abruptly. Alex turns around and scans the classroom, all but a few eyes focused on open text books. He catches Marnie Topper's gaze, but she seems to be staring right through him, which isn't unusual for Marnie. She became a druggie not far into the 6th grade. When she finally realizes Alex is looking at her, she scowls at him and drops her eyes to her book.

"Who was barfing?" a girls asks.

"That's none of your concern, Holly," Mr. Grey says. He's seated in his desk now, reading from the pages of a magazine.

Alex looks at Emma Morgan. She's one of Sarah's friends, but she doesn't appear to be concerned. She must not have seen Sarah run by the door the way he did. Emma's lips move as she reads silently to herself. Her arms are resting on her desk, the fingers on both hands stretching a black elastic hair tie back and forth. He knows in just a few seconds she'll pull her long brown hair away from her face and loop it through the elastic band. He wonders why she wears her hair down everyday. They've shared economics together since the first day of school—Emma's first day at Kalispell High—and she's never made it through ten minutes before tying her hair back. He likes her hair pulled away from her cheeks. He can see her brown eyes better that way, even though she's never really looked at him long enough to allow him to see her eyes.

Alex tries to read from his economics book, but he can't stop thinking about Sarah throwing up in the hallway. He wishes he could've helped her the way a guy might help his girlfriend if she's sick—hold her hair so she doesn't get puke in it, rub her back, whisper that she's going to be okay. Alex has never had a girlfriend, but he's seen a few movies where boyfriends do that sort of thing.

At lunchtime, he waits in line for spaghetti and salad with Dustin Binger, his best friend. Dustin's thin brown hair falls just below his chin, covering the right side of his face as he talks, but

Alex still hears him rambling on about the online match of Bullet Brothers he played last night against some guy nicknamed Beast. Alex is thinking about Sarah again. The senior cafeteria is packed, but she's not sitting at her normal table near the wall of windows. He sees Emma and Randy Cooper, and the three black guys Sarah hangs out with—Reggie Powell, David Brooks and Jalen Parker. Megan Cochran isn't there either. Megan is Sarah's closest friend and the one who drives her home pretty much everyday after school. Sarah used to occasionally come to the gun shop, but not anymore. Even when she did, she wouldn't talk much to Alex, other than to say hello or how are you.

Alex and Dustin sit across from each other at a table on the opposite side of the cafeteria from the table where Sarah and her friends sit, but Alex faces the windows, like he does everyday. He's pretty sure Sarah doesn't ever notice him watching her from so far away. She doesn't notice him anyway. She hasn't really since 5th grade. Sarah was different back then. She wasn't friendly to him just to be friendly, the way she is now. They were actual friends, and she laughed and talked with him the way she does with Randy and Jalen, and David and Reggie. Alex remembers the exact day when Sarah spoke to him for the first time. It was two weeks into 5th grade and Ms. Darby separated the class into reading pairs. Alex and Sarah were placed together. Sarah smiled at him and said, "Hi, I'm Sarah. You're Alex Mackey, right?"

Sarah McKnight knew his name. When the bell rang that day for first recess, she asked if he wanted to play with her and her friends—Alice Jennings, Marnie Topper and Caleb Brown—and for months afterwards, the five of them were always together. But in early May of that year, the Cochran family moved to Kalispell, and Sarah gradually slipped away as she and Megan became friends. Alice moved to Florida that summer, and Marnie decided she didn't want to hang out with just Alex and Caleb. By the mid-

25

dle of 6th grade, she'd befriended a group of girls who wore black lipstick and nail polish and who preferred combat boots over girlie sandals. Caleb and Alex remained friends for awhile, but eventually, Caleb's passion for wresting steered him in a different direction as well. Alex had no interest in sports.

Sarah's still nice to him, but there's a big difference between acknowledging someone in the hallway and inviting that same someone to hang out. The latter never happened after 5th grade, but Alex can't stop loving her. She's the most beautiful girl in the world, and they were friends once, and he wants them to be friends again.

"You gonna eat that?" Dustin asks, pointing the tip of his fork toward the slop of spaghetti and meat sauce on Alex's tray.

Alex shakes his head. "Go for it."

Dustin shovels forkfuls of slimy pasta into his mouth. When he's done, he pushes the empty tray back toward Alex.

"Eat much?" Alex says.

He picks up the tray and rises from the table, turning just in time to accidentally bump into Joe Berger. The side of Alex's tray hits Joe in the stomach. Any other student walking by might've hesitated before saying or doing anything. After all, it was an accident, but Joe's reaction is swift. He hits the bottom of the tray with both of his hands, sending the utensils, the half-empty milk carton, and the tray itself several feet into the air. The leftover milk splatters onto Alex's t-shirt, and the tray hits the wall before crashing to the ground, leaving a slight trail of salad dressing and meat sauce across the floor.

"Watch what the fuck you're doin' asshole!" Joe shouts as he grabs the front of Alex's shirt.

Alex puts his hands up. "Sorry. Sorry."

Dustin remains seated, his eyes glued to the top of the table as though nothing is happening.

"Leave him alone," a voice says.

26

Alex doesn't turn, but from the corner of his eye he sees a small group of students approaching from the left. As they near, he recognizes they're from Sarah's table by the two distinctly different shades of skin color.

Joe loosens his grip on Alex's shirt, and as he steps forward, he pushes Alex back. Alex's leg hits the bench of the cafeteria table, and he falls down and sideways, landing on his hip on the ground.

"Watcha gonna do about it?" Joe asks.

Alex looks up to see David Brooks standing face-to-face with Joe, their noses just inches apart. Joe is slightly taller than David at roughly six feet, but they appear to be equal in weight. They both play football in the fall, and David's currently on the cross-country team. And because Joe and his father are frequent visitors to the gun shop, Alex knows Joe keeps himself in shape post-football in preparation for hunting season's long outdoor excursions. It's not just necessary for when hauling equipment into the woods, but also for carrying the hundreds of pounds of deer and elk carcass back out. Like every other "sport," Alex finds hunting uninteresting. Not so much because he doesn't think it'd be cool to kill a deer or an elk or a moose, but because he prefers the pistols and handguns to the rifles, for no other reason than those are what he uses when playing Bullet Brothers.

Mr. Johnson, the industrial arts instructor, steps between Joe and David.

"Okay, boys," he says. "Knock it off."

"Prick," Joe hisses at David.

Mr. Johnson pushes Joe and points in the opposite direction from where David is standing. "Go." When Joe turns and walks away, Mr. Johnson looks at David. "Best you stay clear of him, Brooks."

As Mr. Johnson leaves, David looks down at Alex. "You okay, man?"

27

"Yeah," Alex replies as he stands.

David bends down and retrieves the tray from the floor. He hands it to Alex.

"Thanks," Alex says.

The bell rings sharply, scattering in every direction the crowd of students who'd hoped to see a fight. And even though Joe is quite possibly the biggest asshole in the entire school, the sides would've been equal. David moved to Kalispell the summer before 11th grade. Like Reggie and Jalen—who'd started 10th grade together at Kalispell High—David was quickly accepted by some, and not accepted at all by others, and all for the same reason. He's black. But unlike Reggie and Jalen, David is a star football player. Sarah's on the soccer team, and she's a skier, and Alex knows she's attracted to David because he's an athlete too. This, more than the color of his skin, is why Alex doesn't like him. He also knows David would've come to anybody's rescue if it meant starting a fight with Joe Berger. Much like Sarah, David is always nice to Alex, but they're definitely not friends.

For many others, however, like Joe Berger, the color of David's skin is exactly why they don't like him. It's why Sarah's father doesn't like him. The reasoning behind this dislike is a mystery Alex has been trying to figure out ever since George McKnight first offered him a job at the gun shop. David had just moved to Kalispell. Sarah and Megan had been hanging out a little bit with Jalen and Reggie, but it wasn't until after David showed up that they all seemed to become such good friends.

"Hurry up, dude," Dustin says. "You're gonna be late."

Alex picks ups the empty milk carton and utensils and sets them on the tray, then places the tray in one of the racks near the cafeteria's kitchen.

"I'll catch you later," Alex says. He points at his milk-soiled shirt. "I need to clean this shit up."

Dustin waves before disappearing into the dispersing crowd.

In the bathroom, Alex soaks a handful of brown paper towels, but the milk stain doesn't dissolve.

"Fuck this," he whispers.

He walks back to his locker and retrieves his books and backpack, then walks out the south doors and into the cool April afternoon. The sky is a crisp blue, clear of clouds and bright with sharp sunlight. The grass across the schoolyard is still brown, but Alex sees shafts of green poking out here and there, patches of blades brave enough to fight the cool temperature and reach for the warmth of the sun. April and May are the teaser months in Montana—sporadic sunny days that bring flowers to bloom, only to kill them again with sudden bursts of rain and snow and cold.

As Alex reaches the sidewalk, he sees Megan's red Honda Civic speeding up the street toward the school's parking lot. She's alone in the car and obviously hoping to make it on time to her first class after lunch, but she's already late. She must've taken Sarah home and left her there. Or, maybe Sarah's at the shop? If she's really sick, she might've preferred to go there than to be alone. Up until last July, she came to the shop at least once or twice each week. Then suddenly, she stopped. As far as Alex could tell, nothing had changed much in the year between starting his job and last summer, but Sarah's father wasn't so sure. He'd asked Alex to keep an eye on her and report back to him anything unusual.

"I know she and Megan have become friends with those black boys, Alex," George had said. "And I can't do much about that. It's the way the world is now, I guess. But…just let me know if anything looks…strange with all of them."

Strange? Alex knew what George meant, but the mere thought of it made him queasy. Since that conversation last summer, he's been honoring George's request, trying not to make it too obvious to Sarah that he's "watching" her, but he only sees her at school.

He's not privy to her life beyond the doors of Kalispell High. But from what he can tell, Sarah isn't going out with anyone. All she's ever cared about is being on the ski and soccer teams, and getting into UCLA in Southern California, which she did. Rumor is, she's never been interested in starting a relationship in high school. That makes Alex happy in one way, but disappointed in another, even though he wouldn't have a chance in hell with her. She's garnered the reputation of being prude, and she's apparently proud of it. But the whole school also knows she's the only daughter—the only child—of George McKnight, and everybody knows George owns a gun shop.

Alex watches Megan run across the parking lot to the front doors of the building. When she disappears, he turns back around and continues walking toward home. Normally, he'd just go straight to the shop, but the milk on his shirt will start stinking soon, and he'd rather change into something clean. George drives him home at the end of each day, but Alex never knows until the moment they pull up to his trailer and George cuts the engine whether he'll be sleeping in his own bed or on the cot in the shop. Only then can Alex hear whether his parents are fighting. If it's quiet, it means his father is already passed out, and Alex can make it to his room without drawing any attention. Otherwise, George drives him back to the gun shop.

If there's a chance of chaos at home tonight, Alex would hate to have to go to school tomorrow wearing the same stained shirt. By then, the stain would be a yellowish green rather than white, and the stench of his sweat mixed with spoiled milk would be too much for even him to tolerate, let alone anybody standing anywhere close to him. Best not to draw any extra attention to himself. Just being a living, breathing entity in the school's hallways is enough to draw ridicule.

Alex has to walk through Sarah's neighborhood to get to the small mobile home park where he lives. As he passes Sarah's house, he keeps his head down as though he doesn't care he's walking by her front porch. Her bedroom window faces the street. He glances up, but drops his eyes again when he sees her blinds are closed. He walks another six blocks before crossing the street that marks the end of Sarah's quaint neighborhood and the beginning of a stretch of smaller, single-story houses, most of which are in need of fresh paint and new lawns. Maple Leaf Mobile Park sits at the end of that stretch—a small pocket of tiny mobile homes and trailers surrounded by an 8-foot cinder block fence. The residences are scattered about, separated from one another by a communal gravel road and carports. Some have small patches considered front yards, three of which are always littered with plastic toys—mostly broken—and children's bikes and scooters.

Alex's trailer is just inside the entrance to the park—the second one to the left. The gravel road passes in front of it, and then loops around the entire complex, making it easy for George to continue driving through the park to get back out rather than have to turn around. Alex lowers his backpack from his shoulder as he steps onto the concrete landing that acts as his front porch. He pulls his house key from the back pocket of his jeans and inserts it into the keyhole in the doorknob, but the door is already unlocked.

Oh, shit.

Alex loses his grip on the knob as the door swings violently open.

"What the hell you doin' home?" his father asks.

What the hell are YOU doing home?

Between the hours of 11 and 5, Alex's father is usually bellied up to a bar somewhere.

"I asked you a question!" he shouts.

31

He grabs Alex's upper arm and pulls him into the trailer, slamming the door behind them. With all of the blinds closed and the lights turned off, the living room is dark, but Alex still sees the four empty beer cans and an ashtray full of cigarette butts decorating the coffee table. The room smells of stale smoke and sour feet. UFC highlights are splashing across the muted television screen, painting a mural of swirling colors on the ceiling and opposite wall.

"Why ain't you in school?"

"I need to change my shirt," Alex says, his stomach twisting into a tight knot.

His father grunts. "What? What the fuck you talkin' about, you need to change your shirt?"

"Why're *you* home?" Alex asks, keeping his voice to nearly a whisper.

His father flips on the kitchen light, spilling hazy fluorescent yellow into the murky living room. "What'd you say to me?"

Alex lowers his gaze to his feet.

"You walk in here an' ask me what I'm doing in my own house!" his father shouts as he steps toward him.

Alex remains still for a moment, wanting to be strong, but he turns and tries to run for the door instead. His father's heavy knuckles catch the side of his head, just below and behind his left ear, and Alex crashes into the television set, knocking it off its stand and onto the floor. A second blow lands on his right cheek and across his nose, sending searing hot pain through his mouth and throat. He tastes the salty bitterness of his own blood. It's not the first time he's been hit by his father, but the blows are usually kept low, away from Alex's face to avoid visible marks. He silently curses himself for not paying more attention to the trailer when he'd walked up to it. He thinks about Dustin's dad, the way he often does when his father is shouting at him or hitting him, and he wonders what it would be like to have a dad who loves him. Alex wants to scream, wants to tell his father to fuck off, but he can't.

As his father raises his fist again, Alex pushes against his chest, sending him sprawling backwards and tumbling into the kitchen. Before he has a chance to get up, Alex grabs his backpack and runs out the front door, blood oozing from his nose and trickling down onto his milk-stained t-shirt.

~3~

My cell phone rings at exactly 3:08. I'm curled into a fetal position on my bed, my phone clutched in my right hand. I'd fallen asleep after Megan dropped me off.

"Hi David," I say as I roll onto my back.

"Hey baby," he replies. "You okay?"

"I guess. Must be the stomach flu."

"Yeah, I heard you left your breakfast in a garbage can."

"Nice, huh?"

"Pretty hot, actually."

I laugh. My stomach growls, so I roll to my left.

"Guess this means you won't be over tonight," David says.

"Probably not."

"Damn. Mom's making her badass jambalaya too, just for you."

Damn is right. I've never tasted anything like Yvette's jambalaya. It's a recipe her grandmother who'd grown up in Louisiana gave her. I'd actually never even eaten jambalaya before being invited to David's house for dinner at the end of last August. Ever since, Yvette's prepared the meal at least twice a month for me.

"And her spicy bacon-wrapped peppers too?" I ask.

"Uh-huh."

"Bread pudding?"

"I'll save you a serving of everything," David says.

"I don't feel so bad right now," I reply. And I don't. In fact, I'm hungry. "Probably not a good idea to eat a bunch of Cajun food, though. Won't taste so good coming back up."

"Yeah. Not so much. All right, baby. Just wanted to check on you. Feel better. I'll text you later."

"K. Love you," I say.

"Love you too."

I set my phone on the nightstand and sit up slowly. I don't want the nausea to come back, and it doesn't. Instead, I'm now starving. I've never had the stomach flu before where I wanted food halfway through it, but right now, I think I could eat just about anything. I make my way down the stairs and into the kitchen where I open the refrigerator—leftover pasta, a loaf of bread, milk. Nausea creeps back into my stomach.

Okay, maybe I can't eat anything right now.

I close the refrigerator and take a banana from the basket on the butcher-block table. I take a few bites, and when I know I won't throw it back up, I eat the rest. As I drop the banana peel into the garbage can, I realize I haven't had the stomach flu since junior high school, and the last time I had it, I pretty much threw up all day. Yvette made brownies last night. Maybe I ate one that wasn't fully cooked.

That has to be it. Raw eggs.

I sink into the sofa and turn on the television. I watch two entire reruns of *CSI* before Dad walks in the front door carrying a pizza box and a brown grocery bag.

"Hey there, sunshine," he says. "Heard you left school a little early today."

He sets the pizza box on the dining room table and empties the grocery bag onto the butcher-block—a head of lettuce, a tomato, a cucumber, a small jar of black olives, and a bottle of Paul Newman Italian salad dressing.

"Oh, yeah," I say, closing my eyes. "And what little birdie told you that?"

"Alex," he replies.

Of course he did.

"Said you puked in a garbage can outside of Mr. Grey's classroom."

I walk into the kitchen, lifting the pizza box cover as I pass the dining room table. The smell of hot melted cheese and spicy tomato sauce is strong, but rather than make me gag, my mouth waters.

"Thin crust pepperoni!" Dad says. "But if you're just gonna barf it up, I'll eat it all myself."

"I feel fine, Dad," I reply. "Pizza sounds really good, actually." Pizza sounds more than really good. I think I could eat the entire thing if Dad let me. I kiss him on the cheek and pat his stomach. "I think maybe *I* should be eating all the pizza."

"Hell, no," he says. "I'm old. I can take it. But just for kicks, I'm gonna make a salad too, with black olives."

Black olives are one of my favorites, but unlike the pepperoni pizza, the thought of putting a salty olive on my tongue right now makes me queasy again.

"So," Dad says, "what happened?"

"Nothing. Stomach flu. It's going around."

"It is?"

I sit at the dining room table.

No. Actually, it's not.

Dad pulls a knife from the wooden cutlery holder next to the sink. He returns to the butcher-block and begins chopping the lettuce, tomato and cucumber. His hands move swift, his eyes wide, his lips pursed.

"You need some help?" I ask.

He doesn't answer. In two quick movements, he dumps the chopped vegetables into the spinner, then steps to the sink, pours cold water onto the salad mixture, and twirls the top of the spinner until all of the water is squeezed out. He dumps the salad into a large glass bowl and sets the bowl and salad dressing onto the dining room table.

"You okay, Dad?" I ask, but I know he's not.

He retrieves two plates, two sets of silverware, and a small stack of paper napkins and brings them to the table as well.

As he sits across from me, he says, "Fine. Why?" He looks at the table. "I forgot drinks."

I rise from my chair. "I'll get it, Daddy. What do you want?"

"I'd love a beer, sunshine, but I'll go with a Coke tonight instead."

Uh oh.

No beer means he's in a space where drinking will only make him angry. I pull two cans of Coke from the refrigerator and sit back down, handing one to him.

"What's wrong?" I ask.

Something is on his mind. I know him too well, and it's not just because he doesn't want a beer. He becomes quiet and distant, his eyes open and watching, but seeing something different than what's in front of him. He sucks his lips into his mouth and pinches them between his teeth, making them pale and thin. And if he's not actively doing something really quickly—like chopping lettuce and tomatoes and cucumbers—he's tapping his fingers against whatever he can tap them on. Usually, his legs.

He scoops salad onto his plate, and then grabs a slice of pizza. He takes a deep breath. "Alex came in today, his face all beat up."

"What?"

For as creepy as Alex is, I feel sorry for him. I wasn't the only friend who deserted him, and by the time 7th grade rolled around, he was pretty much a loner. For most of that year, he kept to himself until Dustin Binger moved to town. I remember being relieved to see the two boys hanging out together. I didn't feel so guilty anymore. But there was so much more than just Alex being alone at school. I can't imagine what it must be like to live in a house like his. The stories are only rumors, but in a city the size of Kalispell, it's difficult not to believe them. I'd never wish that kind of life on anybody, and certainly not on someone like Alex who's already a target at school. I'm always nice to kids like him, but Kalispell High—like any other high school—has its fair share of assholes, and I've witnessed enough bullying to be happy I've never been on the receiving end of it.

"He normally gets to the shop around 3:30 or 4 o'clock," Dad says, "but he showed up today just before one. Blood all over his face."

"Did he get beat up at school?"

Dad shakes his head. "His father." He sets both of his hands flat on the table, his eyes focused on the slice of pizza on his plate.

I have no idea what he's thinking about, but I can guess. His mother died when he was six, and for ten years, he had to deal with his own father beating him up on a daily basis. Dad never talks much about his childhood, but he once told me my grandfather was a constant drunk and "meaner than a pack of dogs".

"Is he at the shop?" I ask.

Silence.

"Huh?" Dad looks up. "Oh…yeah. I'm gonna bring him a clean shirt when we're done eating. I ordered him a pizza too and dropped it off before coming home."

"Okay."

"You ever seen his face all beat up?" Dad asks.

I take a slice of pizza from the box and set it on my plate, trying to remember if I've ever seen Alex with bruises on his face. Surprisingly, I haven't. "I don't think so. There've been stories about his mom, though."

"Yeah. I've heard those too. Alex said his dad slaps him around sometimes, but never…never like this."

I take a bite from my slice of pizza. I'd like to shove two more down my throat, but I don't. I want to makes sure the first round of cheese and sauce and pepperoni are safely secured in my stomach before eating anything else.

"You mind cleaning up, sunshine?" Dad asks as he stands up. He carries his plate to the sink, his salad and pizza still resting on it. "I'll be back in a bit. Just gonna take the poor kid some shirts."

"Sure," I reply.

As I watch Dad hurry up the stairs to his bedroom, I feel an ache in my chest and my throat tightens. For two years, he's been taking care of Alex because he's reminded of his own childhood, and he can't stand watching another person live that lonely life. It's an honorable thing to be doing, and yet, there's this other side of Dad that's dark and secretive, that thinks it's okay to drive around with a sticker on his truck that represents hate and intolerance. And it's this side of him that forces me to keep my own secrets.

I look down at the slice of pizza on my plate, my appetite gone.

∽

For the next four days, I wake up and throw up. The nausea passes by mid-morning, and I manage to get through the rest of each day without puking, but there's a persistent uneasiness that lingers in my stomach. It's not from Yvette's brownies. And it's not the flu.

On Friday after school, Megan and I drive south on Highway 35, through the small town of Bigfork, and on to Polson at the southern tip of Flathead Lake. It's a good 50 or so miles from Kalispell, so there's little chance of anybody recognizing us. I'm not even sure how I'd respond if news got back to Dad that I'd been spotted in Target buying a pregnancy test.

"It was for someone else," I'd maybe say.

But who? And if I used someone else's name, the rumor would spread through Kalispell like a bad bug. It's better just to go elsewhere. Besides, it's just a precautionary measure. That's what I keep telling myself, but the nervous swirl in the pit of my stomach continuous to remind me of the very real possibility I might be pregnant.

As we leave Bigfork, I stare out the passenger window of Megan's Civic at Flathead Lake, roughly 30 miles long and 15 miles wide—the largest fresh water lake west of the Mississippi River. At this time of year, the water is receded far enough away from the shoreline that wooden docks stand naked over the rocks. Boats are hibernating on their trailers, waiting to be to be released back into the fullness of the lake at the start of summer.

Julie Allen, one of my soccer teammates, lives on the west side of Flathead, in a big log home with 300 feet of lakefront and every water toy imaginable. Julie's dad is a surgeon and the chief of staff at Kalispell Memorial Hospital. At the beginning of every soccer season in mid-August, Julie's parents throw a huge party for all of us and our parents, and any friends of ours who are not on the soccer team, including boys. It was at last summer's party that David

40

and I kissed for the first time, hidden in the shadows at the edge of a clump of pine trees separating the Allen's property from their neighbors to the north. There were so many people at the party, nobody seemed to notice when we slipped away.

David walked toward the Allen's house, and then veered to the right. When he was just out of sight, I followed his path, turning around periodically to make sure I wasn't being watched. The moon was full that night, and it painted a pale white path across the surface of the lake, giving me just enough light to find my way. When I stepped beneath a cluster of low-hanging pine branches, David was waiting on the other side. We didn't say anything. I stepped toward him, and when he took my face in his hands and kissed me, I knew I was in trouble. I'd known for months I didn't want to just be David's friend anymore, and I was terrified of my own feelings. I started to notice every time we were around each other my legs would grow weak, my pulse would quicken, my hands would tingle. When we were with our friends, I wanted to be closer to him. I wanted to accidentally brush my arm against his so I could feel the butterflies come alive in my stomach. And when we were apart, I couldn't stop thinking about him. I knew what it meant, but I couldn't act on my feelings. But I also knew David felt the same way. I'd catch him staring at me, and when our eyes would meet, he'd smile and lower his gaze. We denied it for a long time because we knew it was okay to be friends. It was acceptable.

At the intersection of Highways 35 and 93, Megan pulls into the parking lot of the Polson WalMart. She kills the engine.

"You ready?"

"I guess so," I say.

We walk into the cold, bright, noisy warehouse and make our way to the grocery section. A young mom is reading the label on a can of soup, a screaming little boy sitting in the middle of her cart. She doesn't seem to notice the ear-piercing wails escaping from the kid's small lungs. Megan moves past the soup aisle and grabs a box of granola bars and a plastic jar of mandarin oranges from the next.

"That's an interesting combination," I say.

"I know, right?"

I pick out a roll of paper towels, trying my best to forget the real reason we're there. "At least you might actually use these."

We walk past the remaining grocery section and into health and beauty. Halfway down the first aisle, I see the row of home pregnancy tests—five different brands. I feel dizzy.

"Does it matter which one?" I ask.

"Beats me," Megan replies. "I've heard of E.P.T, though. Get that one."

I grab the box and place it between the roll of paper towels and my chest, determined to hide the kit until the very last second before I have to place it on the conveyor belt for the store clerk. As we step into a check-out line, the woman with the screaming boy moves up behind us. The child is now in her arms, sucking on his fingers, his cheeks red and streaked with tear tracks. Both of his nostrils are oozing strings of yellow snot. I look away from him, hoping I won't throw up in the middle of WalMart.

Megan puts her items on the belt, then turns to me and takes the roll of paper towels and the pregnancy kit. From the corner of my eye, I see the woman with the boy staring at the small box as it moves toward the clerk. I look at her, and she turns her face away, but not before I see the sadness in her eyes, a glimpse of pity for me, the girl standing in line who's not much younger and who's just a few years away from carrying her own kid around in the local WalMart, snot crusting around the edges of his nose.

"I need to get out of here," I say to Megan as I push past her and out the automatic doors into the cool air.

42

On the drive back to Kalispell, I open the E.P.T. box and read the small pamphlet inside.

"What's it say?" Megan asks.

"I have to pee on this end of this thing," I say, holding up the test stick. I point to the two small windows in the middle of the stick. "A blue plus sign in this big round window means I'm pregnant."

Silence.

"Holy shit," Megan says.

I put the stick back into the box. "This can't be happening."

Megan places her hand on my thigh. "Let's not jump to conclusions, Sarah. You don't know anything yet."

But she's wrong. I do know. I know exactly when it happened. Two months ago, David's parents flew back to Denver to visit family for the weekend, and his little sister, Rayna, was invited to spend that Saturday night with a friend. David and I had a whole night and a whole house to ourselves. He cooked dinner. We smoked a little of the pot Megan gave me. It wasn't long before we were in David's bed. We'd been having sex since the end of September. I lost my virginity to him the night we went with all our friends to Big Mountain to watch a final summer concert on the hill. He'd turned 18 in July and was able to rent a hotel room in Whitefish. At the end of the concert, everybody went home, but David drove to the hotel, and Megan dropped me off there on her way back to Kalispell. Having sex for the first time didn't feel weird or wrong, like I'd been told. It hurt, and I cried, but David wrapped his arms around me and hugged me to his chest, his lips pressed to the top of my head. There was nothing wrong about it.

On that Saturday night, he was inside me. We were moving together, slow and gentle. We were kissing. And then something happened. It was sudden, but I knew there was something wrong. David shuddered and groaned as he moved away from me, but I

43

sat up quickly, the sticky wetness dribbling out of me and onto the bed.

"Oh my God," I whispered.

"Shit!" David shouted.

For a brief second, the two of us just stared at the torn condom. There was a rip from one side to the other, across the tip. It looked like it was smiling. When David moved again, the rip opened, and I couldn't help but think the damn thing was laughing at me. I jumped from the bed and ran into the bathroom where I sat on the toilet for ten minutes. I took a shower and scrubbed at my vagina with soap, over and over again. Afterwards, I sat back on the toilet for another 30 minutes. I'd heard a story once—a myth—about a girl who avoided getting pregnant by peeing over and over again. It was bullshit, but I didn't know what else to do.

I didn't panic when I missed my last period. I'd been a little irregular ever since starting at 14 years old, sometimes going two or three months without one. Dad said my mother had been the same way.

"Are you gonna call David?" Megan asks.

I told him this morning what Megan and I were doing, and I promised I'd text him when we got back to Megan's house. He wanted to come over and be with me.

Can you meet us at Megan's in ten minutes?

His response is quick.

See you in five.

I cradle the phone in my hand. The wallpaper image saved on the screen is a UCLA Bruin football helmet I downloaded from the school's athletic department website. David will be wearing one of those helmets soon. When he first moved to Kalispell, he was dead-set on returning to Colorado after graduation and playing for UC Boulder. But by the time he and I started seeing each other, he'd already changed his mind. I think I sold him on So-

Cal's sunshine, to the idea of having beaches and mountains not far from campus, and to the massive list of all the things we'd get to do in Los Angeles, like professional sports and comedy clubs and cool stores that would never, ever come to Kalispell. I knew L.A. from television and movies and magazines. I wanted to go there. David sold himself on the UCLA Bruins football program, and they were plenty pleased to offer him a full-ride scholarship based on his grades and athletic ability.

"It's meant to be," I'd said when he told me the news of the scholarship. I wouldn't know about my own acceptance into the school until a month later, but with my grades and SAT scores, I wasn't worried. "As soon as we're out of here, we won't have to hide anymore."

I'd been counting down the days ever since.

I drop my cell phone into the front pocket of my school bag. If I am pregnant, I won't be able to hide it for long. I'll be showing way before leaving for California. How am I going to explain it? Can I even go to UCLA if I'm pregnant? Will David still be able to play football? How are we going to take care of a baby? And Dad? He'll never speak to me again.

I press my fingers against my temples.

"Anything I can do?" Megan asks.

Still rubbing my head, my eyes focused on my lap, I say, "Would you hate me if I got an abortion?"

"Under the circumstances, Sarah, I'm not sure you have a choice."

If I thought I did, I wouldn't have said it. The word doesn't scare me. I know I have the freedom to make this decision, but I'm surprised by how easily it slipped into my head. Just knowing I have the option helps me breathe.

I look at Megan. "That's not what I asked."

She turns to meet my eyes. "No way. I'd do the same if it was me."

When we pull into Megan's driveway, David's silver Camry is already there, and he's leaning against the driver side door. He waves as Megan parks next to him. He opens my door and wraps his arms around my waist when I step out. I clasp my own arms around his neck.

"It's gonna be okay, baby," he says.

Megan's parents are still at work—they both taught at universities in Minneapolis before being invited to run the sociology department at a local community college—and Megan's brother, Chris, is a freshman at Montana State University, so the house is empty. I hold the plastic WalMart bag in one hand, the fingers of my other laced with David's.

"I'm gonna let you guys inside," Megan says, "then I have to take Lou for a walk. You can use my bathroom if you want."

Lou is Megan's family's 13-year-old German Shepherd. Megan's first after-school chore is to take the poor animal for a walk around the block. Luckily for Megan, the walks keep getting shorter and shorter as Lou's arthritis worsens.

As soon as she leaves and the house is quiet again, I take the E.P.T. box out of the plastic bag. While I'm in the bathroom peeing on the test stick, David waits on the other side of the door. It doesn't matter how long we've been together, or what we've done to and with each other, I'll never be comfortable going to the bathroom in front of him, not even someday when we have our own place together in L.A. I think it comes from growing up with no mother and no sisters. As soon as I was old enough to pee on my own, I started shutting the door on Dad.

"I'm done," I say loudly.

David offered to set his watch for ten minutes as soon as I told him I was finished.

"Can I come in now?" he asks.

I open the door. The test stick is resting on the counter next to the sink. I take both of his hands in mine. His fingers are shaking. We sit down together on the edge of the bathtub, but we don't speak. When the alarm on David's watch goes off, we both jump. A line of sweat appears along the edge of his forehead, but I'm freezing. I rise to my feet and step toward the edge of the sink, and as I do, he reaches out and takes my hand, then inhales deeply and drops his head as though he's praying.

When I see the distinct blue plus sign in the big round window, I blink twice just to make sure. I don't know if it's real. There's a sharp pain in my stomach, like I've just been kicked by a steel boot, and I bend over a bit in hopes the movement might get rid of the pain, but it doesn't.

"Oh, David," I exhale.

He stands up and moves toward the sink. A short, airy squeak escapes from his lips, and he squeezes my fingers so tightly, I'm afraid he might break them.

"Doesn't look so bad now," George says.

Alex is staring at his reflection in the mirror above the sink in the small bathroom in the back of the gun shop. His nose and right eye are still a little swollen, but the deep mixture of black and purple coloring has faded some and is now turning yellow around the edges.

"You'll be back to normal in no time." George smiles at him, then walks back through the door and into the shop.

Alex hasn't been back home since the altercation with his father on Monday. It's now Friday, and neither of his parents has tried calling him on his cell phone. It's as though he doesn't exist. They don't care where he is or what he's doing, but it wasn't always this way. Alex does remember times when he was happy, especially with his mother. She's been a beautician at a small hair salon on

Main Street since before he was born. He used to walk there just about everyday after school. He'd grab a small handful of candy and suckers from the glass jar on the counter, smile at Shelly—the 22-year-old high school drop-out hired to schedule appointments until she finished beauty school—and sink into the small, worn-out sofa in the back of the salon to watch his mother shampoo and cut and tease. At 5 o'clock, she'd take him by the hand, and they'd walk the short distance home. He'd tell her all about what happened at school, and she'd fill him in on all the gossip she heard from her clients.

It was mid-way through 6th grade when Alex stopped going to the salon. His father lost his job at the Johnson Creek Timber Company in Columbia Falls after a female colleague accused him of sexual harassment. Alex's mother had to work two jobs after that—a beautician by day and a 7/11 clerk by night. She'd go straight from the salon to the convenience store. She and Alex didn't talk anymore. And his father couldn't find another job— word spread fast about Chuck Mackey. So instead, he took up drinking. It wasn't long before he added hitting to his list of specialties. Alex's mother is the primary target, but Alex also receives his fair share of abuse, nothing he considers too terrible. Nothing that's ever drawn blood, until Monday.

Alex leans over the sink and splashes cold water on his face. The tiny bathroom has a toilet and a shower as well, and is connected to a small room with bare walls and a cement floor. In the middle of the room, pushed against one wall, is a cot with a sleeping bag and pillow where Alex has crashed for the past four nights. A small refrigerator is in one corner, and at the foot of the cot is a 12-inch television sitting on top of two stacked blue milk crates. It's old, but it works. Two more blue milk crates are positioned side-by-side at the head of the cot.

49

When Alex started working at the shop almost two years ago, George offered the room as a safe haven. It's no secret Alex's mother is physically abused by his father, even though she denies ever being struck by him. Alex once saw an episode of *Dr. Phil* where a group of battered women were secretly videotaped being beaten by their husbands, and they *still* denied the abuse. It was right there, on video for all the world to witness, and the women all claimed the tapes were fake. They sat there—two of them with fairly fresh bruises—and defended their partners. Alex tried to help his mother at first, but the more he pushed, the more she turned her back on him, so he stopped trying.

Alex wipes his face with the small hand towel hanging on the shower door, then replaces it and sits at the edge of the cot. On Monday night, George brought him some t-shirts so he'd have something clean to wear to school. On Tuesday afternoon, he not only stocked the small refrigerator with food and bottled water, but he'd swung by Target and picked up new socks and underwear for Alex, soap and shampoo, and a toothbrush and toothpaste. He'd even given him a pair of sweats to wear so he could take Alex's bloodied t-shirt and jeans home to wash.

Alex didn't go to school on Tuesday—George thought it best if he stayed at the shop, alternating frozen packs of peas on his face until the swelling subsided some. He wanted Alex to go the principal on Wednesday and report his father. Instead, when Mr. Borlain confronted Alex about the obvious battle wound, he said a guy he didn't recognize had jumped him in an alley near the mobile home park.

"This didn't have anything to do with what happened in the cafeteria on Monday, did it?" Mr. Borlain had asked.

"No, sir," Alex replied. He could've lied and said yes, but then Joe Berger would've added even more black and blue coloring to his already painted face.

Alex has his own reason for denying his father's abuse. Unlike his mother, or the women on *Dr. Phil*, he doesn't want to tell the truth because he wants to handle the situation on his own somehow. He's tired of being weak. So tired of it.

"Hey sport."

Alex looks up to see George standing just inside the small room.

"I'm closing up. You wanna help me put some things away?"

"Sure."

As he rises from the cot to follow George, Alex glances at the door at the end of the room opposite the bathroom. Above the small iron handle on the left side of the door is a padlocked latch. George once told him there was a storage room behind the door, for outdated guns and ammunition, but on one of the nights a few months ago when Alex stayed at the shop, George came in late and went into the room while Alex pretended to be asleep. George left the door open an inch, so Alex crept up and peeked through the crack. He didn't see boxes of what would be outdated guns and ammunition. In fact, the side of the room he could see was empty, but the wall was covered with newspaper clippings and photographs, one overlapping the other. From where he was standing, Alex couldn't read any of the articles, but most of the photographs appeared to be of individual and groups of black people. He also recognized several black and white pictures of Ku Klux Klan members and burning crosses. When George's shadow moved across the room, Alex crept back to the cot. George came out a few minutes later and secured the padlock before he left.

Other than having a Confederate flag bumper sticker on the back of his truck, George doesn't appear to be what Alex would expect a KKK member to be. In his American history class last year, Alex watched a documentary on the civil rights movement. The director interviewed a number of Ku Klux Klan members, their faces shielded behind white flaps of cloth and pointy hats, their eyes appearing wide and blazing through the holes cut in the cloth. They were yelling and chanting, using words such as "nigger" and "coon". George is nothing like that. He's funny and kind. All he ever does is gloat about Sarah, and other than the Kalispell residents who don't believe in the right to bear arms, George is generally liked by everybody. He smiles at every customer, even the ones who don't deserve a smile.

"Can you put those two back where they belong," George says, pointing at two guns on the display case. "I'm just gonna finish with the daily log."

Alex nods. The guns are a Springfield XD 357 Pistol and a Springfield Tactical XD 357 Pistol. He picks up the smaller, non-Tactical gun and points it at the glass cabinet doors behind the display case. Inside the cabinet are two rows of rifles. Alex sees his hazy reflection through the glass—the yellowing bruise, the slightly swollen nose, his dark eyes and thick eyebrows like his father. He pretends to aim and shoot the weapon.

"You know how to handle one of those?" George asks. He's standing at the cash register near the front of the shop, counting dollar bills and stuffing them into a tan bank bag.

Without looking at him, Alex says, "Can you teach me?"

~

Alex finishes the last of the burrito George brought him from Qdoba, then tosses the empty container in the trash before brushing his teeth. He crawls into the warmth of the sleeping bag and flips through the channels on the small television—local news, *Two and a Half Men* reruns, a drastically cut version of the movie *Heat* on TNT. It's at the final scene when Al Pacino chases Robert De Niro into a field outside of the LAX freight terminal. Alex tries to identify the type of gun Pacino carries, but the scene takes place at night and the setting is too dark.

George had hesitated when Alex asked whether he could teach him how to use a gun.

"What for?" he'd asked.

"I don't know," Alex replied. "I think I'd like to be a cop someday."

The thought of being a police officer had never actually crossed Alex's mind before, but he figured it was better than saying, "Cause I hate my dad and I wanna kill him."

"Sarah's never been interested in shooting a gun," George said. "I guess if I'd had a son, that might've been different."

He left for home, but returned a few hours later with food for Alex.

"I'll pick you up at eight tomorrow morning," he'd said. "There's a shooting range out on Highway 2. We'll take a Glock 19. It's the most common with law enforcement."

On the television, Pacino shoots DeNiro, and Alex smiles. He doesn't think he could really kill his father, but something about knowing he could if he wanted to—that he'd actually know how to successfully do it—makes his hands tremble. He closes his eyes and imagines walking into their dumpy little trailer and seeing his father hitting his mother, her screams leading a macabre orchestra of howling neighborhood dogs. With the Glock held firmly in his right hand, Alex raises the weapon. In slow motion, his father turns. He hasn't shaved in days, his eyes are bloodshot, his skin seeps the pungent odor of sour whiskey. Blood from Alex's mother's nose is dusted across his already dirty t-shirt. Alex holds the gun steady, the nose of it just inches from his father's forehead.

But then Alex isn't standing in the tiny living room of his trailer anymore. He's sitting in the cafeteria at school, surrounded by a sea of unfamiliar faces, all of them looking at him and laughing or whispering, pointing their fingers in his direction. The Glock is still gripped in his right hand, hidden under the table. He feels the hot metal against his skin. Across the cafeteria, sitting at the table near the wall of windows, are Sarah and David. They're the only two people there. Sarah gets up to leave, but David grabs her by the wrist. She tries to pull away from him, but he won't let go. When Alex sees she's crying, he stands from the table and walks toward her, the gun shaking in his hand as he presses the nose of it to David's temple.

At 7:45, the alarm on Alex's cell phone wakes him. *Heat* has been replaced by a rerun of *Law and Order*. He turns the television off and dresses quickly. As he's tying the laces on his tennis shoes, he hears the familiar ringing of the little bell above the front door of the shop.

"Up and at 'em, kid!" George yells.

Alex grabs his cell phone and windbreaker off the milk crates at the head of the cot and walks into the shop. George is unlocking the sliding door from the display case closest to the cash register. He takes out a Glock 19, then closes the door and relocks it before tucking the tiny key into the breast pocket of his red and blue flannel shirt. He puts the gun in a black case with three cartridge magazines, closes the case, and turns to Alex.

"You up for a quick breakfast?"

"Sure," Alex says, his stomach bubbling with excitement as he stares at the gun case.

He follows George out of the shop and jumps into the passenger seat of George's truck parked at the curb. Main Street is quiet, but it won't be long before early morning Saturdays aren't so still anymore. By late June, Kalispell will be crawling with summer tourists. The season is good for most of the businesses, especially the antique stores, the galleries that feature local artists, and any of the shops that offer souvenirs. But for George, the mass of non-residents who come to the state to enjoy its most precious resource (the west entrance to Glacier National Park is a mere 30 minutes away) aren't stopping by to see him, unless it's the occasional gun collector who discovers he can avoid paying sales tax by purchasing from George.

As the truck pulls away from the curb, George says, "How'd you sleep?"

"Pretty good." Alex thinks about his dream. His father. Sarah. David. His hands are damp.

"I know it's not the most comfortable sleeping arrangement, but—"

"Beats going home," Alex says. "I really appreciate the help, Mr. McKnight."

At the Highway 2 junction, George turns left, heading west. He continues for roughly a half mile before pulling into a McDonald's drive thru. He orders two Sausage McMuffins with Egg, a black coffee, and a large orange juice.

"I know I've told you about my own father," George says, not moving his eyes from the windshield. "My life wasn't much different than yours, Alex. That's why I've been helping you."

"I kinda figured that."

"And if somebody hadn't come along and helped me out...well, I don't know where I would've ended up."

The woman in the drive-thru window smiles, revealing a large space between her two front teeth. George hands her a ten-dollar bill. She gives him the coffee and orange juice, then the bag of food. As she passes him his change, she says, "Have a lovely day."

"You too, darlin'," George says.

She blushes.

Alex opens the bag and removes both of the breakfast sandwiches. He hands one to George.

"Anyhow," George says, "the guy who helped me...his name was Clive Sanders. He taught me a lot, but it wasn't until after he showed me how to use a gun that I felt safe. From everything, you know."

Alex takes a bite of his sandwich, the grease from the sausage dribbling down his chin. No, he doesn't know. Other than occasionally pretending to aim and shoot a gun while he's restocking the weapons at the shop, he has no clue how to use one. And if not for George giving him a place to hide from his father, he'd never feel safe.

"When you asked me last night if I could teach you," George continues, "I wasn't sure. I mean, I don't want you doing something stupid."

"Stupid how?" Alex asks.

George devours his sausage and egg muffin in four big bites, then takes a sip of his coffee.

"I guess if you have to ask, I shouldn't be concerned," he says, smiling. "I know for me, I just wanted to be able to defend myself if and when the time came."

Alex continues to eat his breakfast, his eyes moving back and forth between his food and the passenger window. He'd give anything to be able to defend himself.

"Sarah's heading off to UCLA at the end of the summer," George says. "She's a smart girl, Alex, but she don't know how dangerous the world can be. There're people out there who could hurt her, and all I've ever tried to do is protect her and show her how to protect herself. She just doesn't seem interested. And rightfully so, I guess. She didn't have my life."

Alex crinkles up the paper his breakfast sandwich was wrapped in and stuffs it into the empty food bag. "She's really lucky, Mr. McKnight. To have you."

George takes another sip from his Styrofoam coffee cup.

"She's been acting real strange the last few nights," he says. "I know she hasn't been feeling too well, but…I don't know. She got home around ten last night, and I could tell she'd been crying, but she didn't want to talk about it. She went to her room and didn't come back out. Said she'd been at Megan's house since school got out, but when I called over there to find out from Megan what happened, Megan's mom said she'd gone to Whitefish with her dad. They weren't gonna be home until late."

Alex drinks the rest of his orange juice and adds the empty cup to the McDonald's food bag. His face feels hot. Sarah must've lied to George, but why? He doesn't deserve that. She has no idea how fortunate she is.

"All we've ever had is each other," George says. "It just seems like this past year, she's slipped away a little bit, and I don't know why. Maybe it's because she's a senior. I don't know."

They pass the remaining businesses at the western end of Kalispell—a Chevy dealership, a Lowes, a Murdoch's Ranch and Home Supply. Past Murdoch's is a seemingly endless yellow pasture speckled with patches of brown and white cattle, their heads bent to the ground. In the distance is a two-story white farmhouse, partially hidden by a row of massive maple trees planted years ago to provide some shade for the house's residents. Beyond the amber landscape to the north is Big Mountain, the ski runs looking like long white strips of carpet between clusters of green.

Alex had gone to that farmhouse once with his mother, not long after she'd started working two jobs and their walks together ceased. The family of one of her clients owned it. She'd asked for a shift change at the 7/11 so she could take Alex there to pick out a puppy from a litter of mutts that'd been born eight weeks before. Alex was so excited he could barely sit still in the car. When they pulled into the dusty driveway of the farmhouse, a short older woman in a long blue skirt and white apron waved from her porch and pointed to a weathered brown barn just behind and to the right of the house. Inside the barn was a border collie mix and six fat puppies.

Alex grabbed the biggest and fattest of the puppies and held it to his chest while the tiny animal whined and licked his face. On the drive home, the puppy fell asleep in his lap. But Alex's father wasn't so happy to see the dog, and while Alex waited in the car, he listened to his parents screaming, his mother crying, and then his father stormed out of the trailer and ripped the puppy from his lap. Alex doesn't know what happened to it. He never saw it again. And after that, his mother never picked him up from school again either, never took him anywhere, and after awhile, stopped paying much attention to him altogether.

"You sure you haven't seen anything unusual?" George asks.

Alex turns away from the window and looks at him. "Not at school, but I don't see her much anywhere else, so it's hard to tell."

George's lips drop into a tense frown. "I know she's going to some fundraiser thing tonight for the school. She mentioned it earlier this week."

"It's a fair," Alex says, remembering the flyer he received yesterday during first period. "The school does it every spring. It's at the gym. Anybody who's involved in a group activity, like sports or yearbook. 4H. Whatever. They all have a booth where they sell different stuff, like food."

George looks at him. "Are you going?"

Alex isn't a member of any group. "I hadn't planned on it."

George frowns and looks back at the road. Alex has never participated in anything related to the school. He's never been to a dance or a party. Never gone to a football game or basketball game. And he's never gone to the spring fair. Why would he? Having to go to school everyday is bad enough. No need to offer himself up for additional bantering.

But now Alex thinks about the bizarre dream he had last night—Sarah and David alone at the table, Sarah crying. Probably, it means nothing. Sarah's a common visitor to him in his dreams. He's woken up from them many times with a painful erection, not because they're erotic in any way—although he can't deny letting his imagination go now and then—but because in them, Sarah loves him. He doesn't always remember how the dreams play out, but when he wakes up, there's a brief recollection of feeling wanted. It's only after the fog of sleep lifts that the harsh reality of his life drops on him like a bag full of bricks.

Alex sees the pain in George's face—the heavy eyes and sad mouth, skin hanging from his jowls like the gravitational pull of the earth suddenly intensified. It's a look he's never seen on George, and it makes him angry. Sarah is keeping a secret from her father, and Alex can find out the truth. He just has to make the effort. For all George has done for him, it's not much to ask.

"I can go tonight, Mr. McKnight."

George turns to him again and smiles. He places his right hand on Alex's shoulder. "I'd so appreciate it, kid. I never thought I'd be a spying dad, but I've also never given Sarah a reason to hide anything from me." He puts his hand back on the steering wheel and slows the truck in order to turn left onto a gravel driveway. He parks in front of a long, single-story brick building with a door and no windows. "I hate to see her hurting. Whatever it is, it must be pretty bad. I just need to find out what…or who."

"I'll find out what's going on, Mr. McKnight," Alex says. "I promise."

"Thanks," George replies. He pulls the keys from the ignition and sets his hand on top of the black gun case between them. "Now, why don't I show you how to use this thing?"

59

~5~

I stay in bed until nearly noon on Saturday. When I finally get up, I run straight to the bathroom and puke. I picked at Yvette's roasted chicken at David's house the night before, but that had been around 7 o'clock. I haven't eaten anything since, so there's nothing in my stomach but sour yellow bile. It burns my throat and tongue.

Yvette had made a comment about my appetite.

"Since when do you not eat a meal of mine?" she asked.

David placed his hand on my knee. "She hasn't been feeling too good the last few days."

"You do look whiter than normal," Rayna said from across the table. She smiled at me.

"You better watch it, young lady," David's dad said.

"I'm just kidding," Rayna whined before scooping a spoonful of peas into her mouth.

"You better be kidding," I said, "or I'll come over there and breathe all my sick germs on you."

I was hoping to keep the three of them from thinking there was anything wrong besides a case of the stomach flu, but I could feel Yvette's eyes on me, her lips stretched tight and thin across her teeth.

Did she know?

Rayna giggled, letting three small peas escape from her mouth and drop back onto her plate.

When David and I were alone again in his bedroom after dinner, I tried not to cry, but there was no holding it back. I'd been sobbing since Megan's, but managed to stop a good 30 minutes before we got to David's house. At the dinner table, it took every ounce of energy I had not to lose it again. Later, when David dropped me off two blocks from my house, just before ten, I'd hoped I could make it to my bedroom without Dad seeing my red and swollen eyes, but he was lying on the sofa watching television when I came in. As soon as the questions started, I bolted up the stairs and to my room.

"I've been at Megan's all afternoon, Dad," I said. "I'm just tired."

I brush the bitter taste of bile from my mouth and walk downstairs. I see a note on the dining room table and pick it up.

Hope you're feeling better, sunshine.

Shop opens at noon if you want to come down.

Otherwise, I'll be home after 5:00.

Love, Dad

When I was little, I spent just about every Saturday afternoon at Dad's shop. I didn't have much of a choice. There wasn't anyone else around to take care of me. My mother, Laura, left just two months after I was born. She'd been the oldest of eight children, and because of her own mother's death at a young age, ended up raising her brothers and sisters as though they were her own. She was 32 years old when her youngest brother finally turned 18, and when he graduated from high school, she left the small town of Ashford, Alabama and moved to Birmingham where she met Dad. They were married within a year. At 35, she found out she was pregnant with me. She wanted an abortion, but Dad promised if they kept me, he'd take full responsibility so Laura could live her life. I guess instead of risking the possibility she might get stuck raising another child, she up and left. We never heard from her again.

The only other relative Dad's ever mentioned is a girl named Alice, but he only spoke of her one time. When I was in 4th grade, my teacher, Mrs. Thompson, gave us the assignment of making family trees. I didn't really have a family, so instead of a family tree, she said I could make a collage out of childhood photographs of Dad, along with childhood photographs of me. Since I'd never seen any pictures in the house except for the framed ones of Dad and me together, I decided to snoop in his bedroom in hopes I'd find some baby pictures of him. But the only photograph I found was in the top drawer of his bedroom dresser, and it was of him and a girl with long dark hair. They both looked to be about 14 or 15 years old. When I later showed the picture to Dad and asked who the girl was, he stared at the black and white photograph for a few minutes, his eyes appearing glazed over as though he was looking through the picture rather than at it, and then he tucked it into the pocket of his shirt.

"That's my sister. Alice," he'd said.

I remember feeling excited. Dad had a sister? I had an aunt?

"She's dead," he continued.

The excitement disappeared. No wonder he'd never mentioned her before.

"How'd she die?" I asked.

Dad stood up then and walked out of the dining room and up the stairs. Without looking at me, he said, "An accident."

Alice was never spoken of again, and the photograph disappeared. It had always been just Dad and me, and although there'd been some nights—as well as a few Saturday afternoons—spent with babysitters or friends, for most of the years when I was too little to be left alone, Dad had been there to take care of me. He'd been the only disciplinarian, the only homework helper, the only set of ears when I needed someone to talk to. He brought me to Big Mountain every weekend when I was little so I could learn to ski. He showed me how to play soccer. He came to all of my school activities—concerts, sports, parent/teacher conferences. He was even the one who sat down with me when my period started and explained the birds and the bees.

"A lot of good that did," I say.

My chest feels like it's being squeezed by a giant pair of pliers, but I fight the urge to cry again. I grab the note from the dining room table and crumple it into a small ball, then throw it across the kitchen. It hits the ground and rolls a few feet before stopping. I don't know why, but I suddenly feel like it's mocking me as it sits there in a little heap, the words scribbled on it completely unaware of what's going on inside my body. I run and grab the note and throw it again, over and over and over until I have to lean with my hands on my knees to catch my breath.

My cell phone rattles against the dining room table where I placed it when I found the note. I toss the crumpled ball of paper into the trash and retrieve the phone. There's a new text message from Megan.

What time should I pick you up?

The girls from the soccer team had planned on meeting at the high school at 5:30 to start setting up our booth for the spring fair.

If Megan picked me up at 5:20, we'd easily make it to the school by 5:30, but the note from Dad said he'd be home after 5 o'clock. I didn't want to see him.

Can you swing by a little early? Like 4:45?

Sure thing. See you at 4:45.

I eat a plain Eggo waffle and half a banana. As I'm setting my plate in the dishwasher, my phone rings.

"Hi David," I say.

"Hey baby. How you doing?"

"As good as I can be, I guess."

"You think you'll feel up to talking to my parents tomorrow afternoon?"

I close the door to the dishwasher and take a deep breath. As soon as David saw the blue plus sign on the pregnancy test stick, he insisted we tell his parents. I barely had time to digest it myself, let alone run to Yvette and Clarence with the news. David told me a long time ago he could never keep anything from his mom and dad.

"They can see right through me," he'd said.

As much as I hated lying to Dad, I had no choice. Yvette and Clarence don't care whether I'm black, white, orange, green. They don't see the color of my skin the way Dad sees theirs.

"Do we have to tell them?" I ask.

David's hesitation answers my question.

"I can't keep this from them, Sarah," he says. "But I know they'll support us. You know my dad. He's all about education and waiting to start a family. And Mom's sister had two kids before she was 19, and she's a mess. Mom always says Aunt Sade should've aborted those two."

"She says that because their brats, David, and she's only kidding." I bite at my lower lip. "And you don't think they'll say anything to anybody?"

"Hell, no."

"Did you find a place?"

"Yes," he replies. "There's a clinic in Missoula. I talked to a lady there this morning. She said there's some paperwork to fill out, a health questionnaire, and an exam, but since you're 18, it'll be easy. She also said if you're less than nine weeks, you can have a medical abortion instead of a surgical one."

I place my free hand on my stomach and close my eyes. He sounds so educated about it, like he's been studying abortion procedures his whole life. I'm dizzy, so I sit down at the dining room table.

"You take two kinds of medication," David says. "One at the clinic and another 72 hours later at home. The lady said it's sort of like having a miscarriage."

I see myself sitting in a bathroom, blood and tissue and discharge and whatever else seeping from my vagina and dripping into the toilet. When it's all out of my body, do I just flush it away, down through the bathroom pipes and out with all the rest of the sewage? My stomach turns.

"And how's that supposed to be better?" I ask, a thin line of sweat breaking across my forehead. I keep thinking maybe I'll wake up from this nightmare, that the barfing and the trip to WalMart and the little blue plus sign are all just figments of my imagination, that tomorrow I'll wake up in my bed and it'll be Monday morning again, and everything will be like it was before.

David sighs. "I don't know, baby. But I'll be with you through all of it."

My face is warm. "You'll be with me through all of it? What're you gonna do, David, jump into my body?"

Silence.

"I'm not the one who thought of this, Sarah," he says.

My hands shake as stinging hot tears fill my eyes. I try to speak, but my voice catches in my throat.

"I'm so sorry, baby," David says.

I'm sobbing now. It *was* my idea. I didn't even ask him what he thought. But he wants to be a football star, and we both know getting there is a battle without having a kid to take care of. And I have my own dream. I want to be a doctor, a pediatrician, and it's a long, tough road from undergrad through medical school. I want to go where David and I will be accepted, where our children will be accepted. I want three kids someday—two boys and a girl. I want a house with a swimming pool and a big backyard where we can barbecue with friends, and where all of the neighborhood kids can come over and play. I know it'll take time to make all of our dreams come true. It'll take time to be accepted the way we want to be accepted. Having a baby now will make all of it—everything we've ever wanted—impossibly out-of-reach.

"It's not your fault, David," I say. "And I'm sorry too. I never even asked you for your opinion."

He takes a deep breath.

"Ever since I got offered my scholarship, all I can think about is us going to California," he says. "We can't be together here, Sarah. I don't expect things to be perfect down there, but I know they'll be better than here. I get so excited when I think about all the things we're gonna do. I just…I just don't wanna screw any of that up. And I'm…I'm not ready to be a dad."

In his bedroom the night before, when I brought up the idea of getting an abortion, David didn't outwardly agree or disagree, and he didn't say much about it in the car on the way to dropping me off. I thought he felt differently, but I hoped he didn't. Hearing his words now melts the tension in my neck, like butter on a hot pan. For the first time since yesterday afternoon, I don't feel like there's a pair of hands trying to push me into the ground.

"I gotta run, baby," he says. "Randy's trying to call through. He needs help bringing some stuff to the gym for the football booth. Let's sneak down to the middle school tonight and talk, okay?"

"Sure," I say.

"I love you, Sarah McKnight."

I wipe the tears from my cheeks. "I love you too."

∼

"You don't look so good," Megan says as I drop into the passenger seat of her car.

"I'm pregnant, Meg. How am I supposed to look?"

She frowns. "Sorry. That was a stupid thing to say." She looks behind her shoulder for oncoming traffic. The street is quiet. As she drives forward, she says, "I just can't believe it. Are you sure you don't wanna get another test? Just in case. Or maybe you should go to a doctor, to be sure. Those tests aren't always accurate, you know."

I sigh and look out the window as we pass through my neighborhood. There's the elderly Gershon couple with their little green lawn and white-picket fence, Mr. and Mrs. Avery with their mailbox painted like an American flag—Mr. Avery is a retired Marine, a survivor of the Vietnam War—and the Matthews family with their pansy-lined walkway leading to a covered front porch where their golden retriever, Nugget, always lays like a rug with his face drooping over the edge. I sometimes babysit the Matthews' three boys— Aaron, Michael and Robert. They're six, four and 18 months. The Matthews family attends the same church as Dad and me, always dressed as though their post-church plans include a professional family photo shoot. If they ever found out about David, about me being pregnant, they'd probably leave the church, sell their house, and have all three boys (and Nugget) sterilized, just in case.

67

"I'm pregnant, Meg," I say. "I don't need another test to prove it. I know when it happened."

She sighs. "Okay."

"We're going to Missoula on Monday morning, first thing," I say. "David found a clinic. I'm pretty sure I'm less than nine weeks, so I can take some kind of pill, and then another one a few days later. And that's it. It'll just…come out, I guess."

Silence.

"Well…that's cool," Megan says.

And that's exactly what I want her to say. Cool. Done. Let's move on. Megan's my best friend because we're peas-in-a-pod, two-of-a-kind. If she were the one pregnant, I'd have the same response. Go get the abortion and come home. We're graduating in two months. Let's enjoy the summer, and then get the hell out of here. Who cares how cute your baby would've been. Who cares if you spend the rest of your life wondering if you made the right decision. Even if Megan wanted to say those things, she wouldn't. She wouldn't because she knows I wouldn't.

"Just be careful down there," she says instead. "There's always a bunch of pro-lifers picketing outside of those clinics. They hate you, and they don't even know you."

Hate me?

"I didn't try and make this happen, Megan. It was an accident."

She stops at the red light at the end of the street and turns to me. "I know that. But it doesn't matter to those people. They won't care about your story. But ask any one of them if they'll take your baby instead of you having an abortion, and I bet they'll all say no." She holds my gaze for a brief second, and then looks back at the stoplight.

"How do you know all this?" I ask.

The light turns green, and as Megan drives forward, she says, "My cousin, Annie, had an abortion two years ago. My Aunt Jane's daughter. You know, my mom's sister."

I nod. I'd met Jane and Annie a few summers ago when they came out from Minneapolis to visit. It was the summer before Annie's senior year of high school. She was three years older than Megan and me.

"Annie got pregnant by some guy she met at a fraternity party in Chicago," Megan says. "They were both really drunk. She barely knew him. She didn't know what else to do. She was really upset. She said there was no way she could have a baby, and she didn't want to quit school to go through the pregnancy for an adoption. She was really scared. Mom and Aunt Jane and me all talked to her about getting an abortion. It was really the best thing for her. She was a mess."

Megan turns left at the next street. "So she goes to this clinic referred to her by a counselor at the college, and there were all these people standing around with signs. They weren't all yelling at her, but some were, calling her a baby-killer and that she was the daughter of the devil, that God would punish her."

I take a deep breath against the rising lump in my throat. "What'd she do?"

"She had the abortion."

I sigh and let my head fall back against the headrest.

"She's fine with it," Megan says. "The abortion. She knew it was the right thing to do. But those people fucked her up, Sarah. The things they said to her. The way they treated her. She said she'd never felt so low in all her life. They called her a dirty, baby-slaughtering whore. And they were carrying around Bibles and preaching about God. Like God would want anybody treated that way."

Megan pulls into the high school parking lot and into an empty spot near the front entrance to the building. She kills the engine.

"Annie's been going to therapy." Megan turns to me. "Not because of the abortion. Because of those people. I'm just scared for you is all."

I look down at my hands, ghostly white in the hazy light of the late afternoon sun. My life will never be the same. I knew it the minute I saw the little blue plus sign. It doesn't matter how easy the physical abortion might be—swallow a pill, then another, sit and wait for a period, heavier than normal, some cramping. It's still an abortion, the removal of what would've been my baby. I'll have to live with that for the rest of my life, no matter how many other children David and I eventually have. And like Annie, I'll have to hear the taunts, the ridicule, the insults. I'll have to walk through the rest of life knowing there are people out there in the world who hate me for what I did, for what I felt I had no choice but to do. I'll go to bed every night, hearing their voices, and wondering about the child I aborted.

So, what if I keep the baby? My life will still never be the same, and there's no candy-coating what our future will look like—the both of us trying to go to school full-time, having to work in between hours to make ends meet, David having to quit football to help support a baby. I'll have to postpone medical school, maybe indefinitely. And what about Dad? Without having the baby, there's still a glimmer of hope that someday he might come around and embrace my relationship with David. Maybe, someday.

There's a knock on the passenger window. Megan and I jump. It's Emma.

"Move your butts, girls!" she shouts, her voice muffled. She turns and runs to join three of our soccer teammates walking toward the front doors of the school.

I reach across the console and grip Megan's hand. I'm scared, and she knows it, but I want her to see that I'm strong.

"I'm gonna be fine, Meg," I say.

The palms of Alex's hands are still a little red, and when he presses the tips of his fingers together, there's a remaining numbness he wonders whether or not will ever go away. The funny thing is, he doesn't care if it stays. He and George were at the shooting range for almost four hours, and they were the best four hours of his life—not because he learned how to shoot a gun, but because George made him feel like he was important enough to spend four hours of his time teaching him how to shoot a gun. Not since before his mother started working two jobs has Alex felt this way, and even she never made him feel this important.

It took awhile for Alex to get comfortable with the Glock. It was heavy and bulky in his skinny hands, and when he pulled the trigger the first few times, he thought the damn thing was going to go straight through his palm and snap his wrist. But George coached him all morning on everything he needed to do—proper stance and grip, sight alignment, breath control, trigger squeeze. By the time they left, Alex felt as though he'd been shooting a gun his whole life.

They stopped at A&W for burgers and fries and root beer before arriving back at the shop just before noon. Business was slow throughout the day—just a few of George's repeat customers came and went, mostly to purchase ammunition for target practice, and Kyle Burton needed a new scope for his rifle for a black bear hunting trip planned for mid-May. Kyle is always friendly to Alex. When George told him they'd spent the morning at the shooting range teaching Alex how to properly use a gun, Kyle suggested learning how to shoot a rifle next.

"Then you can come along on my next outing and see how it feels to shoot a moving target," he'd said. "Nothing beats bringing down a big beast like that."

When George left the shop just before 5 o'clock, he kept the Glock out so Alex could practice dry shooting. By six, Alex had already shot the weapon almost 200 times. He didn't want to stop, but before George left, he told him to take it slow, suggesting no more than 150.

"You can bump it up to 300 tomorrow, sport," he'd said. "You'll already be a little sore from the morning."

But Alex doesn't feel any pain, other than the mild numbness in his fingertips. In fact, he feels strong, energized…alive. He feels exactly how George told him he'd feel—safe. He understands he can't walk around with the Glock tucked in his jeans or hidden in his backpack, but just knowing he could shoot it properly if it was in his possession gives him a sense of pride he's never felt before. When he was shooting at the bullseye target board in the range, he'd imagined seeing a photo of his father's face pinned to the center of it, then Joe Berger's, and then a handful of other assholes at his school who'd used him as their own bullseye target over the years. He thought of his dream the night before—of how much he wanted Sarah to love him—and he remembered how upset George had been, so he imagined David's face there too.

There's no mistaking the infatuation between Sarah and David. Alex has tried convincing himself he's paranoid, but he's been watching Sarah long enough to see it all—the prolonged stares between the two of them; David's hand briefly resting on her back before sliding down and brushing across her butt; Sarah's leg pressed against David's under the cafeteria table, as though nobody can see. And most everybody doesn't see because they're not trying to. But Alex is, and he does. Ever since George asked him to keep an eye on Sarah, he's avoided the possibility of there being anything romantic between her and David, and he's chosen not to reveal to George any of the "strange" things he's seen. This is in part because Alex wasn't sure if what he was seeing was real, or just his mind playing tricks on him. It didn't seem possible. Or, more importantly, Alex didn't want it to be possible.

Now, staring down at his hands, the redness in his palms almost completely dissipated, he accepts the truth. And he does so because, for the first time since Sarah turned her back on their friendship at the end of 5th grade, he has something to impress her with. He's still ugly, athletically challenged, and skinny, but that's just on the outside, and there's absolutely nothing he can do to alter these genetic mishaps. But on the inside, the kid who gets picked on at school and beat up at home no longer has to sit back and take the abuse. He can defend himself just as easily as any of the jocks or the coked-up metal heads, and not because he's physically strong or psychologically whacked out on drugs, but because he can now hold, aim and shoot a gun with deadly precision and accuracy. How many of the motherfuckers in his school can say that?

The Glock is resting on the cot next to him. It's a black, oddly shaped chunk of polymer with a steel slide. It's not a living, breathing entity, and yet Alex feels a strange connection to it, an admiration. He doesn't want to leave the weapon here, but he knows George would be pissed if he found out he'd even considered tucking it into his backpack and taking it with him to the school fair. Alex realizes he doesn't have the key to the gun cabinet, so he puts the Glock in its case and slides the case under the cot.

He checks the time on his cell phone. It's just past 7:30. The fair started at 7 o'clock. He dials Dustin's number.

"What's up, dude?" Dustin says. "Thought we were gonna get together this afternoon for some Bullet Brothers?"

"Yeah, sorry about that," Alex replies. "I had some shit to do this morning."

"Did you go home?"

"Fuck, no. I still haven't heard a word from my parents."

"Shit," Dustin says. "Sorry, dude."

"I'm better off staying here, believe me."

"Yeah, but you can't stay there forever, right?"

Alex hasn't really thought about it. He's stayed at the gun shop sporadically for the past two years, but never for more than two consecutive nights. He's been here now since Monday, and George has paid for everything (and taken Alex's dirty clothes home twice to launder). He also gave Alex $20 this afternoon in case he wanted to buy some food at the fair. George won't be able to take care of him forever, and Alex will eventually have to go home and confront his father.

"I'll stay as long as I can," he says.

"Well, why don't you come over to my house tonight," Dustin says. "Jason's coming over too."

Jason Maxwell is a junior, a nice enough kid, but a video game junkie, and even though Alex enjoys playing Bullet Brothers with

Dustin, it does get kind of old after the first few hours. The last time Alex went to Dustin's house when Jason came over, Dustin and Jason stayed up until five in the morning playing video games.

"I'm actually thinking of going to the school fair," Alex says.

Silence.

"You're kidding, right?" Dustin asks.

"I just wanna get outta here for a little bit, and I don't feel like sitting around. I might just walk over there and check it out, and then walk back."

"All you, dude. Come by later if you want."

"I guess that means you don't wanna go?"

"Um, let me think about it," Dustin says. "No." He laughs. "Why the hell do you wanna go to the school fair? Are you okay?"

Better than okay.

"Yeah," Alex replies. "I'm fine. I'll come over later."

They say goodbye, and Alex tucks his cell phone into the back pocket of his jeans. He puts the key to the back door of the shop in the front pocket of his windbreaker and zips the jacket up. Without Dustin, he'll definitely be an odd sight at the fair. If asked, he could say he's helping one of the teachers, but who? He doesn't even know which teachers are assisting which groups. By the time he gets to the school, it'll be dark enough where he might be able to linger outside without drawing too much attention. At this point, all he can do is try.

Alex leans forward. "Who the fuck cares what they think."

He wants so badly to reach under the cot and take the gun, tuck it between his stomach and his jeans, feel the heat of it against his belly. The thought of it being there, within his grasp where he could pull it out and press the nose of it to the forehead of whoever might bug him, gives him a sudden erection. He thinks about touching himself, but changes his mind.

No time for that now.

75

He stands ups and walks out of the room, through the back of the shop and out the door leading to the alley.

~

By the time Alex reaches the school, dusk has settled and all that remains of the sun is a brilliant streak of crimson across the western horizon. He thinks the band of red looks like blood spilled across the darkening sky.

Both sides of the street leading to the high school's main parking lot are jammed with cars, which means the parking lot itself is full. He isn't surprised. He's been told the spring fair always draws a big crowd, about equal to the football games. Of course, he's never been to either, so he personally wouldn't know. But the more people, the less attention he'll draw, and once inside, if he stays close to the crowd, he should be left alone. The gym will be packed with not only high school students, but their families as well. In front of parents, most kids behave differently than they do at school, as though the separation is a catalyst for their secret bi-polar disorders.

Alex cuts across the east schoolyard and walks along the northern edge of the building, avoiding the main parking lot and the mass of people walking in and out of the high school's front doors. The gymnasium is located just inside the doors, to the left, the majority of it jutting out into the west portion of the schoolyard. On that end of the building are two sets of double doors that will be open, primarily for fresh air, but also for smokers. The school has a strict policy about smoking in front of the building, including the sidewalk and stairwell leading to the main parking lot, and the parking lot itself. There are four massive stone ashtrays lined up along the outside west wall of the gymnasium, for use during school hours and whenever there's an event held at the gym. Alex will encounter a handful of people mingling about the smoking area, puffing on cigarettes and swigging from hidden flasks tucked inside of jackets, but his plan is to hug the wall and slip quietly through one of the double doors.

When he reaches the northwest corner of the building, he peeks around the edge of it. He's relieved to see a smaller than expected group of people, most of them adults. Further in the distance, he sees a cluster of high school kids, but with the bloody streak of fading sunlight now washed from the sky, he can't identify who they are. He decides to wait—the front of his body pressed against the cold brick wall and just a sliver of his face visible—to see whether the group of students will continue moving away from the building or suddenly choose to go back inside.

An adult in the crowd starts walking toward the stone ashtray closest to where Alex is standing, so he turns around and presses his back to the wall in order to keep himself concealed. As he does this, he sees a single figure emerge from one of the senior cafeteria doors below and to his right. The figure sets off the motion sensor light directly above the door, making it possible for Alex to see who it is before she moves quickly away from the high school and toward the middle school a few hundred yards away.

Alex remains still as Sarah half walks, half runs across the north schoolyard. As she nears the middle school, she turns left and walks along the south edge of the building toward the outdoor basketball courts and soccer field behind it.

"What's she doing?" he whispers to himself.

The motion sensor light above the cafeteria door is activated again. Alex turns and sees David standing beneath the hazy white.

No fucking way.

David tucks his hands into the pockets of his jacket and moves away from the school, nearly following the exact steps Sarah made just minutes before.

Alex's stomach clenches, followed by a sharp pain in his chest. He looks back to where Sarah had just been. She's gone, slipped through the gate in the chain link fence that surrounds the soccer field and courts. During the week, that gate is padlocked to keep any straggling high school punks from messing with the younger kids, but on the weekends, the school agreed to remove the lock so families living in the surrounding neighborhoods could use the space. As long as nothing was damaged and all garbage was placed in the proper receptacles, the school would continue to allow access.

David turns left and continues to follow Sarah's path along the edge of the building toward the chain link fence. When he slips through the gate, Alex walks in the direction of the middle school. He feels his feet on the ground, hears the orchestra of voices and music spilling from the double doors of the high school gymnasium, but the pounding of his heart and the rush of blood in his ears makes everything else seem distant, almost dreamlike. When he reaches the southwest edge of the middle school—the meeting point between the building and the chain link fence—he presses his back against the wall and holds his breath.

Alex knows where they are. The school's library faces the basketball courts, and between the library doors and the strip of grass that separates the courts from the school is a round, open-air courtyard. In its center is a large bronze statue of a bighorn sheep on a circular cement base. In the fall and spring, when the weather is warmer, tables are set up in the courtyard for the students to sit and eat their lunches, and many of them end up sitting on the statue's base. Sarah and Megan used to sit there all the time, at the end facing the basketball courts, just below the animal's massive head.

Alex doesn't want to see what Sarah and David are doing beneath the statue, but he has to. He made a promise to George. He moves toward the gate in the fence and slips through, then cuts to his right until he is again touching the building. He creeps to the edge, the courtyard and statue just around the corner, and stops. He hears David's voice.

"I know it's gonna be tough, baby, but I'll be with you the whole time. And when it's over, I'll still be with you. I'm not going anywhere."

Sarah is crying. Alex bites at his lower lip.

"We were so close," she sobs. "So close to getting out of here and having a normal life together, and now this. I know it's the right thing, David. I know it, but it doesn't change how shitty I feel."

Alex moves a little closer to the edge of the building, just far enough so he can peek at the couple without exposing too much of his face. They're sitting on the cement base just beneath the bighorn's head—exactly where he expected to find them—facing away from him. Sarah is sitting with her back against David's chest, her left foot on the ground, her right leg bent as though sitting cross-legged. David's arms are wrapped around her, his chin resting on her shoulder.

"They have a support line we can call anytime," he says. "This isn't supposed to be easy."

The circular design of the courtyard aids in carrying their voices to Alex's ears. He hears them as clearly as if they were standing right beside him.

"We'll have other babies, Sarah. When we're ready to be parents."

Alex covers his mouth with one hand, not sure if he's trying to stifle a gasp or prevent himself from throwing up. He presses his back against the brick wall, dropping both of his arms to his sides, and squeezes his eyes shut. He's hot, then suddenly cold as the thin layer of sweat on his body soaks his t-shirt.

He needs to get out of here. He hurries back through the gate and cuts sharply left, then runs full speed along the side of the building and around the front, determined not to stop until he reaches the gun shop.

~7~

"Did you hear something?" David asks.

He stands up and walks toward the edge of the courtyard. I didn't hear anything, but I follow him, scanning the basketball courts and soccer field before looking toward the gate in the chain link fence. A knot forms in my stomach when I see the gate is open.

I grab David's arm. "Did you close that?"

"Shit," he whispers.

He takes my hand, and we walk toward the fence and through the gate, closing and latching it behind us. We peer into the darkness to the left, then in front of us. I turn back toward the courtyard. Nothing.

Oh please, no.

"Somebody was spying on us," I say.

"No way. Probably just someone looking for a place to make out. They heard our voices, and they left."

"What if they saw us?"

David takes my face in his hands. "There's no way, baby. Don't worry." He kisses me. "You go back. I'm right behind you." But I feel his fingers trembling against my skin.

I run across the north yard of the high school, my heart pounding, and up the hill to the back of the gymnasium. I try telling myself David left the gate open, that the sound he heard was nothing, but I know he closed it. I know it.

Somebody was spying on us.

Near the double doors, a crowd has gathered beneath a thin veil of cigarette smoke, the cloud hovering above their heads like a swarm of tiny insects. My heart is banging like a hammer in my chest. I don't look at any of the smoker's faces as I slip past them and into the gym. The crowd has grown since I left, their voices nearly drowning out that of Beyonce blaring from the loudspeakers mounted high at each corner of the gymnasium. I squeeze my way through the mass of people until I reach the girls' soccer booth. Megan and Kasey Denton—the tallest girl on the team at 5'11"—are busy selling chocolate chip cookies and double-fudge brownies to a group of 7th graders. Emma is standing near the back of the booth waiting for our shift and flirting with Randy Cooper.

I check the time on my cell phone. It's 8:19. Emma and I are on the 8:30 to 9 o'clock shift together. I walk around the front of the booth and stand next to Randy.

"Ms. McKnight," he says. "Where you been all my life?" With his right thumb, he lifts the brim of his cowboy hat and smiles. "Where's that hunk of a black man of yours? Your pops didn't get to 'em, did he?"

"Very funny, Coop," I reply. "No, Dad didn't get to him. He'll be here in a minute."

"Better be," Randy says. "Hell if I'm gonna stand in that damn booth alone selling cupcakes shaped like footballs."

I look back toward the double doors in hopes of seeing David, but the sea of mostly unfamiliar faces—an expanding mass of eyes and lips and noses, coming and going, moving awkwardly together like a herd of confused cattle—are all white. I see Mr. Kemp, the special education teacher and varsity tennis coach. He's walking with his wife, Doris, and their daughter, Veronica. Veronica's in 8th grade. She makes eye contact with me and holds my gaze. I met the girl once at a soccer tournament. She plays on a junior city league, but we don't really know each other, and yet Veronica doesn't look away from me, as though she knows something—something I don't want her to know.

I look at Emma, and then back at Veronica, but the girl is gone. *Was she the one spying on us?*

Two women—Marge Adams and Lori Brunson—are buying M & M rice crispy treats from Megan. Marge has owned a small bookstore two blocks south of Dad's shop for the past 30 years. She's in her late 60's. Every Monday, she brings Dad a Styrofoam cup of coffee from Buck's Diner on the corner, and they chat briefly before going about their days. I like Marge. When I was little and had to hang out at the shop on Saturdays, I'd walk to her store and she'd let me sit in the back and read books.

"Can't be much for you to do at your Dad's except hang out with a bunch of smelly men looking at guns," she'd say with a laugh.

As Marge hands a dollar bill to Megan, she looks at me, but she doesn't smile and say hello like she normally does when she sees me out in public. Instead, she just stares, her pale eyes unflinching and cold like an angry cat.

Was it Marge?

I cross my arms over my chest and look at my feet.

You're just seeing things, Sarah. Stop it.

I look back at Marge, but now she's talking to Lori Brunson. When Megan hands her a rice crispy treat, she catches my eye and smiles and waves enthusiastically as though she hasn't seen me in years.

"Hello, sweetheart!" she shouts. "Your dad here?"

I wave back. "No. You know how he is with crowds."

Marge nods. "Tell him hello."

"I will."

Now I'm fucking paranoid.

"You okay, McKnight?" Randy asks. He and Emma are staring at me.

"Fine," I say. "I think I'm just seeing things."

"Coop's got some whiskey in his shirt," Emma says. "I know you don't drink, but you look like you could use a swig."

For the first time since the beer bong nightmare, I actually consider the offer. A small sip of Jack Daniels—Randy's preferred choice since his dad keeps at least three bottles of it in their liquor cabinet—might be just what I need to take the edge off.

"Sure, why not," I say.

Randy and Emma look at each other.

"Seriously?" Randy asks.

But then I think about the baby growing inside me.

The baby?

In the 28 hours since I first saw the blue plus sign, I hadn't considered the pea-size embryo to be anything other than "the pregnancy". Deciding against a sip of Jack Daniels happened suddenly, as though my body responded on its own to the possible attack without any input from me.

This is bullshit.

I grab Randy by the arm and pull him behind the booth. Fortunately, our soccer team was given one of the spots along the gymnasium wall rather than a central spot where booths were set up back-to-back. There's just enough space behind our booth for Randy and me to stand side-by-side against the wall and take several quick swigs of JD without being seen. I gasp from the sting of it, but as the hot liquid slides down the back of my throat and into my stomach, I close my eyes and take a deep breath. The alcohol moves through my bloodstream like wildfire, and my toes begin to tingle. I don't care about the baby, the pregnancy. I can drink what I want, when I want to. I can go outside with the smokers and inhale their sickly second-hand death plumes. It doesn't matter because on Monday morning, I'll be free. I'll wake up on Tuesday and go to school, and David and I will pick up where we left off before all of this. And at the end of the summer, we'll be gone.

"Gotta go to work now, honey," Randy laughs.

He removes his hat to kiss me on the cheek, then drops it back onto the mess of brown curls on his head before tucking his hands into the pockets of his Wranglers. As he walks out from behind the booth, he jumps up and clicks the heels of his cowboy boots together. I wonder if Randy's mom drank when she was pregnant with him. As he walks away, his legs slightly bowed at the knees, my mouth goes dry and tears creep into the corners of my eyes.

"It's 8:30," Emma says as she pops her head around the corner. "We're up."

~

At the close of the fair, after all of the volunteers have carted away the wood and paper from the booths, Emma, Randy, David and I wait together in the parking lot until the final car leaves. Dad called twice between 9 o'clock and ten to confirm I'd be home by midnight. I told him I was getting a ride from Emma, which was my original plan all along since Megan had to leave early, but Emma managed to get herself drunk on Randy's Jack Daniels, so he took her keys away.

"Looks like the coast's clear," Randy says. "Best I take this little lady home." He winks at me.

Emma snatches his cowboy hat from his head and puts it on her own.

"I reckon he be right," she slurs.

Randy playfully grabs her by the wrist and pulls her to his chest. They laugh together, and then just smile, and then kiss. It's not the first time they've kissed, and it probably won't be the last before the end of the summer when Randy leaves for Bozeman and Emma goes back to Seattle. I think about how easy it is for them to be kissing in the middle of the parking lot, and even though it's empty, it makes me angry because I know they could be doing it without a worry in the world even if the parking lot was jam packed and full of wandering eyes.

David touches my arm.

"Let's go," he whispers.

We walk to his car without holding hands, just to be safe. I can't shake the feeling we're still being watched, and if we are, I can use Emma's drunkenness and need to be driven home by Randy as an excuse for why David is giving me a ride home.

Two blocks from my house, David pulls to the curb and turns off the lights and engine. The neighborhood is dark except for a handful of porch lights, including mine. Dad is lying awake, waiting to hear the front door open and close, but it's 11:30, and he won't call again unless I'm not standing in the foyer of our house at midnight.

"You gonna be okay?" David asks.

I nod.

"I didn't see anybody, baby," he says. "Maybe it was the wind."

I shake my head. "There wasn't any wind, David. What're we gonna do if somebody knows?"

"We're taking care of it, Sarah. Even if somebody heard us, there's no proof. And after Monday, there definitely won't be any proof."

My throat tightens as tears pool in my eyes.

"You thinking of changing your mind?" he asks.

My bottom lip quivers. I don't want to cry again, but I can't help it. I haven't changed my mind, but the more time I have to think about what's happening to us, what's happening to me, the harder it is to convince myself we're making the right decision. A fuzzy cloud of unknown is swirling around inside my head, and the further we get from first seeing the results of the pregnancy test, the darker and heavier that cloud becomes.

"I'm just scared, David," I say. "I'm scared of somebody knowing. I'm scared of getting an abortion, but I'm even more scared of *not* getting one. I'm scared of how I'm gonna feel when this is all over and of what other people are gonna think of me. I just wish we could leave." I can't stop the tears from falling now. "And tonight, I actually thought about our baby. I thought about it *being* a baby, and it makes me so angry because I wish we could keep it, I really do, but I know we can't, and I'm confused, you know. I'm confused."

David leans across the console and gently pulls my head toward him. He presses his lips against my temple. "I know you're not looking forward to this, Sarah, but my parents will help. They'll know what to do. I'm scared too, baby. But I know everthing'll be okay. I know it."

I turn my face to his and kiss him. I want to stay with him tonight, want it to be like it was just one week ago, before the sickness, before the little blue plus sign. I want to feel the delicate touch of his fingers on my bare skin, taste the sweetness of his lips. I want to lay my head on his chest and listen to him sleep. But even if I could go with him, it won't be the same. It'll never be like it was one week ago. And now it seems the struggle of keeping our relationship a secret, the frustration of not being able to love each other in front of people, and the uncertainty of what Dad will do if he discovers us…it all seems so incredibly simple in comparison to what we're dealing with now.

"You gotta go, baby," David whispers.

"I know."

I kiss him one more time, then step from the car and hurry down the street to my house.

~

I manage to make it into the shower before my morning vomit session, hoping the sound of running water will mask the gagging noises that escape from my throat. When I open the bathroom door, I hear the voices of the commentators from Dad's Sunday morning programs. The volume on the television downstairs is at near maximum, loud enough for the neighbors to hear, so I'm safe.

In Dad's truck on the drive to church, I wish for the morning to move at a snail's pace. If someone *had* been spying on us last night, the news would've spread to the members of Kalispell's First Baptist Church before anyone else. For whatever reason, any taboo information about the teenagers who attend First Baptist seems to always get to the church's members first, as though some invisible policy had been set up long ago. It happened just a few months ago when Leslie Frie—smarter than me with nothing less than an A+ in every class since elementary school—got a DUI after running a red light on Main Street. Nobody ever suspected Leslie to be a partier, especially the members of First Baptist. I haven't seen her at church since.

"How was the fair, sunshine?" Dad asks.

I don't look at him. "Fine."

"You're awfully quiet. Everything okay?"

I nod. The silence that follows is stifling.

"What was all that commotion about on the news this morning?" I ask, hoping the sudden change in topic will steer him away from asking anymore questions. It works, but as he tries to fill me in on the country's latest unemployment numbers, I tune him out.

During church, I don't hear one word of the sermon either, but I study the faces around me, watching their lips move with 'Amens' and 'Hallelujahs'. Although I've attended church more Sundays than not, Dad never made it a "must do" in our lives. There are no bibles in our house, no wooden crosses hanging on our walls. We don't pray before we eat, nor sit on our knees beside our beds at night, fingers folded together, to thank the Lord for all our blessings. On Sunday mornings, we get up and drive to church, sit and listen to the sermon and sing songs, and chat with other members during coffee hour. Then, we go home. I believe in God, and sometimes I privately pray at night. I think Dad might do the same, but we've never really talked about it.

Nobody in the church is looking at me. Their eyes are focused on Pastor Tom with his thick gray hair and coke-bottle spectacles. His deep blue eyes look like fat marbles behind those glasses. Whenever I see him, I think of a cartoon skeleton with bulging eyeballs. The Matthews family is sitting in the pew in front of me, and little Robert keeps turning around and smiling. He's not yet two, so he's squirrely during church—stand up, sit down, stand up again, hug his mom's head, smack his older brother. Normally, I'd make funny faces at Robert to keep him entertained, but seeing him now makes me think of tomorrow morning, and my chest aches, my eyes sting, and I have to look away.

At one point in the sermon, Pastor Tom makes a comment about gay marriage, and I feel mildly grateful he doesn't say something about bi-racial marriage. He doesn't agree with either, and neither do many members of the congregation. I wonder what would happen if I suddenly stood up and announced I was pregnant with a black boy's baby and that we were driving to Missoula tomorrow morning to get an abortion.

After church, I stand with Dad during coffee hour as he mingles with other church members—John and Susan Matthews, Marge Adams, Kyle and Elaine Burton. None of them treat me differently. As I look around the crowded room and see that nobody is whispering and staring or pointing at me, I begin to believe it might've actually just been the wind last night after all.

I sneak off to the bathroom twice, my nausea getting stronger with each passing minute. I'm just moments away from having to sit in front of David's parents to tell them we're in trouble. I see their faces, their dark eyes heavy with disappointment. I hear Clarence sigh and watch him clasp his hands together, his knuckles paling as he clenches his fingers.

On my way back to the church hall from the bathroom, I see Dad talking on his cell phone just outside of the coffee room. As I near, he snaps his phone shut.

"I gotta go over to the shop," he says. He rubs the top of his head.

"Is everything okay?" I ask.

"Yeah. It's just Alex. He seems pretty upset. He said yesterday he might go home this morning and check on his mom. Might've seen his dad instead. I don't know."

"Okay," I say. "Well, Megan's picking me up here in twenty minutes, so you don't have to worry about me. I'll be home by 4 o'clock."

He nods, and then gives me a hug. "I feel like I haven't seen you in days." He steps back and places his thick hands on my cheeks. "I think a couple homemade hot fudge banana splits are in order for tonight. Whaddya say?"

I smile. "Sure, Daddy."

Megan drives me to David's house. As she pulls into his driveway, he walks out the front door to greet us

"Good luck," Megan says. I step from the car. "Text me when you're done, I'll come get you. We'll go over to Little Charlie's." She waves to David, then backs out of his driveway.

"Are they ready?" I ask.

He wraps his arms around my neck and holds me against his body. I smell a mix of spicy deodorant and Bounce dryer sheets. I press my face into his shirt, inhale the sweet scent, then turn my ear to his chest and listen to his rapidly beating heart.

"I sat with them after breakfast and said you were coming over here," he says, "that we needed to talk to them about something really important."

"And?"

"Mom asked if you were pregnant."

I back away from him and look into his eyes.

"She already knew," he says. "She's a nurse, Sarah. She can see these things. Said she knew it on Friday night when you barely touched her chicken."

I take a deep breath, and as I do, I feel my muscles letting go a bit, relaxing with the release of the anxiety that had been building since Dad and I left the house. I know David's parents being aware of my pregnancy doesn't change our situation, but I feel relieved nonetheless.

"Are they mad?" I ask.

"Not mad, really. Just disappointed. In me, not you."

"But it's not your fault. It's not even really *our* fault."

"And they get that. They understand. Things happen sometimes, and that's part of life. Mom said it's how we learn. Dad was pissed at first 'cause he thought I might throw my scholarship away, but I reassured him that wasn't gonna happen."

"Do they know? About the abortion?"

"Yes," David says. "And they agree it's the best option for us right now…and not just because of college."

I feel a sinking sensation in the pit of my stomach. "Dad."

"I realize he's never done anything to me or my parents, Sarah, but he hates us. He doesn't physically *have* to do anything. Did you know he walked right by my dad on the street a few months ago, and he wouldn't even look him in the face. Just walked right by like my dad wasn't even there. Like he didn't exist. He hates us 'cause we're black. Doesn't even know us." David cups my face in his hands and looks into my eyes. "So, it doesn't matter if we have a baby now or ten years from now, he'll never be okay with it. You said it yourself. That's why we're leaving, and I'm not sure we'll ever be able to come back. He'll eventually find out, you know that. And then what?"

I place my hands over David's, remembering the warmth of Dad's fingers when he held my face back at the church. Homemade hot fudge banana splits, always with one scoop of French vanilla ice cream and one scoop of strawberry and topped with honey-roasted peanuts. We started our Banana Split "Sundays" when I was in 1st grade—the first year of being in school from 8:15 to 3 o'clock, Monday through Friday. Saturdays were shop days, as well as the occasional birthday parties and play dates, and eventually, soccer games and skiing tournaments. Sunday mornings were for church, so Dad set aside Sunday nights for hot fudge banana splits. It was our time together, to talk and laugh, play games, watch movies. I can't remember the last Sunday night I spent with him. Weeks ago. No, months. Last summer, maybe.

"I love him," I say.

And I do, more than I've ever told him or showed him. I can count on one hand the arguments we've had. He's never raised his voice to me, no matter how red his face would get when I'd push his buttons, especially during those treacherous middle school years when I sometimes felt forced to choose between my friends and him. But in the end, he always won, and not just because he's my dad, but because I wanted him to win. I preferred going to movies with him and ordering the jumbo pack with double-buttered popcorn and two boxes of candy—always Skittles and Junior Mints. I preferred our father/daughter dinners twice each month at Spiagi's Italian Kitchen where we'd split a dinner for two of thin spaghetti with Momma Spiagi's homemade red sauce and monster Italian meatballs. I even preferred spending Friday nights at home with him, watching old reruns of *Seinfeld*. I didn't choose to hang out with Dad out of guilt. Rather, I chose to spend time with him because he's my favorite person in the world.

"I haven't been fair to him," I say. "I feel like I've turned my back on him, and I know he's confused. I can see it."

"You haven't turned your back on him, Sarah," David replies. "Maybe someday you'll feel like you can tell him about us. And maybe someday I'll get to see the part of him you love so much. Maybe he'll look *at* me rather than *through* me."

But I know this will never happen. I wrap my arms around David's waist and drop my forehead against his chest. "We're doing the right thing."

He kisses the top of my head. "Yes. We're doing the right thing."

~8~

Alex rubs at his tired eyes. They burn. They always burn when he doesn't get enough sleep, but it's not just the lack of sleep now that makes his eyes hurt. He spent hours staring up at the dark ceiling in the back room of the gun shop last night, rehearsing what he was going to say to George. Every time he tried closing his eyes, he'd hear David's voice and see his naked black body pressed against Sarah's, and his eyes would pop back open. He'd gaze at the ceiling, unblinking, until tears spilled down his cheeks, making two small wet spots on his pillow.

Alex sits at the edge of the cot, waiting for the familiar ring of the little bell above the front door of the shop. Fifteen minutes had passed since he called George. He made it sound urgent. He didn't want to risk that Sarah might come along, although he doubts she will. She'd have no reason to come here, especially on the one day of the week when the shop is closed. But his reason for not wanting her here is not just because of the secret he plans to reveal to George, but because his anger toward her makes his hands shake, and he's afraid of what he'd say to her if she showed her face. He felt it throughout his entire body when he ran from the middle school to the gun shop last night—pins and needles jamming into the soles of his feet, his heart nearly exploding, hot tears like fire water scalding his cheeks. When he finally arrived at the shop, he took the Glock out from under the cot and pulled the trigger so many times he couldn't feel his hands for several hours afterwards.

Alex never would've had a chance with Sarah, but it doesn't take away the pain of knowing she and David love each other, that behind closed doors and with lights dim, they make love. Sarah touches David, and he touches her. Their lips have tasted one another's, over and over and over again. And now she's pregnant. If David had never moved here, it never would've happened. From the conversation Alex heard last night, he knows they plan to end the pregnancy, but that's just to solve the immediate problem, to make it look like there never was a problem. It doesn't change the fact that Sarah and David are leaving together, running off to California where they'll eventually get married and have children. And George has no clue. Sarah is his whole world, the reason behind the rising and setting of the sun, and yet she disrespects him as though he's nothing—the way Alex's father disrespects Alex.

At the sound of the little bell, his heart skips. When he stands, he feels weak.

"Alex?" George says as he walks into the small room. "You okay? What's going on?"

He has the same pained expression on his face he had in the truck on the way to the shooting range the morning before—heavy eyes, the skin around his mouth dangling from down-turned lips. For a second, Alex considers not telling him about Sarah. George is a big man. News like this could cause a massive heart attack.

"Is it your dad?" George asks.

Alex suddenly realizes George isn't expecting information about Sarah, even though they'd discussed Alex going to the spring fair to spy on her. Why would he expect bad news? Sarah has no reason to lie to him. He's been a faithful, loving father since she was born, since her mother left the both of them when Sarah was just two months old. George has devoted his entire life to taking care of his little girl.

"Our relationship is special," he'd said to Alex once. "Nothing will ever come between us."

But David *has* come between them.

"You look like you're gonna be sick, kid," George says. "Sit down here and tell me what the hell's going on."

Alex sits back down at the edge of the cot next to George. His hands are shaking against his knees. "I was at the fair last night. I overheard Sarah and..." He swallows, the back of his throat burning.

"You overheard what, Alex?"

"I overheard Sarah talking to...talking to David Brooks."

"The black boy? The football player?"

"Yes."

George crosses his arms over his chest and looks at the floor. "What? What did you hear?"

Alex's stomach burns. "They're together. You know...together." He keeps his eyes on his fingers spread out across his knees.

George stands up and puts his hands in the pockets of his khaki pants. "What makes you think they're together, Alex? I'd know this."

Alex looks at him. "I guess they've been hiding it. I don't know how long, but...long enough to...to..."

"Spit it out, Alex!"

Tears well in Alex's eyes. "She's pregnant, Mr. McKnight. She's pregnant." The words gush out of his mouth like water from a broken faucet. He's sobbing, tears streaming down his cheeks and dropping onto his shirt and jeans. He wipes at the snot building at the edges of his nostrils. "I'm so sorry, Mr. McKnight. I'm so sorry I heard them. I wish I hadn't, but I did. I love Sarah. I love her."

Alex drops his eyes to the ground. He wants to look up, but he's too scared. He flinches as George places his hands on his shoulders, his grip firm and almost painful. Alex wonders whether he might hit him, but then his fingers loosen and he turns and walks out of the small room and into the gun shop. Silence. And then the sound of George crying. A minute passes before Alex hears the crash of broken glass as George smashes one of the display cases. In between shouts of rage is the sound of George's collection of framed photos of the great Montana outdoors being shattered. There are at least twenty of them hanging on the walls throughout the shop. The battle continues for a few more minutes before silence once again settles over the place.

When George walks back into the small room, Alex doesn't move. George's face is streaked red with drying tears. He wipes at his nose with the back of one thick hand. In the other hand, he holds a small key. He turns toward the door opposite the bathroom and inserts the key into the padlock dangling from the latch above the small iron handle.

"Come in here, Alex," he says as he removes the padlock and pushes the door inward. "I wanna show you something."

Alex doesn't move. George disappears behind the door into the dark room. Light flutters, then burns steady as he flips the switch that controls a set of fluorescent bulbs in the ceiling. Alex rises and walks slowly into the room, the wall he saw a few months ago still adorned with newspaper clippings and photographs. Pushed against the opposite wall—the side he couldn't see before—is a desk with a computer and a printer resting on it, and a bookshelf crammed with books and magazines, in what appears to be no particular order. A small black filing cabinet is shoved beneath the desk.

George is sitting in the chair at the desk, his back to Alex. Without turning around, he says, "My daddy ran with the KKK. Had been for years. He used to take me to all kinds of gatherings when I was a kid, after my mother passed away. I was six when she died." He takes a deep breath. "My daddy was a mean son-of-a-bitch, Alex. Drunk all the time. I was 13 when I met Clive Sanders at a KKK meeting. My face was all black and blue from my daddy beating on me. Clive came up to me and started talking to me, and the next thing I knew, he was taking me with him everywhere. Taught me how to stand up for myself, how to shoot a gun. I'd never been around anybody who gave that much of a shit about me. I moved out of my daddy's house and in with Clive and his little sister, Alice, when I was 16."

He spins slowly around so he's facing Alex.

"Clive was 23 years old, taking care of his baby sister," he says. "She was my age. Their parents died in a car accident five years before. They became my family."

Alex crosses his arms over his chest and looks down at his feet. Seeing George's face makes him suddenly uncomfortable.

"Alice was walking home from school when three black boys started following her," George says. "We went to the same damn high school, but me and Clive took that day to go shoot wild turkeys. She didn't have a chance against them. They were drunk, all three of them in their mid-20's. Big sons of bitches. They took their turns with her, then left her for dead in an abandoned warehouse six blocks from home."

George leans forward in his chair. He clasps his fingers together and rests his elbows on his knees. "They were arrested and jailed, but Clive got to 'em anyway. Don't know how, but he was deep into the KKK. Deeper than I'll ever know. Two days later, he was shot outside of a Birmingham club. I went to visit him in the hospital. Just before he died, he asked me to honor him, and to honor Alice, and to never forget what happened. Alice has been living in an institution since the rape. Her brain's complete mush from the beatings."

He stares at his hands, his mouth turned down.

"I dropped out of school and lived on my own for awhile doing odd jobs for different people," he says. "Eventually, I started working for a guy named Brad Placid, one of Clive's buddies who ran a gun shop out of Birmingham. He was the biggest underground supplier to the KKK. I worked for him for over 20 years until he got busted and the place was shut down. That's about the time I met Sarah's mom. I didn't want to raise my daughter around all of that, so I left. Came up here. No fucking black people. Quiet."

George looks up at Alex.

"But I owed Clive my life," he says, "and I couldn't sleep knowing I wasn't doing anything for him. I wasn't honoring him or Alice. I was up here, hiding out with Sarah, pretending I could forget all about of it. That's when I opened the shop." He stands up and nods at the computer, then points to the filing cabinet. "Got my whole operation right here. Been supplying guns to the KKK down south for 17 years." He looks back at Alex. "Trucks come in and out of here in the middle of the night all the time, but nobody thinks twice about it. I have my regular incoming shipments, but I also have a fleet of drivers who bring empty boxes in and carry full boxes out. For 17 years, nobody's ever questioned me, Alex. And why should they? I'm the single father of an only daughter, and I've never bothered anybody. Hell, I don't even have a speeding ticket on my record."

Alex's mouth feels like scorched sandpaper. He swallows, but the sticky dryness in the back of his throat makes him cough. He'd heard the trucks on several of the nights he stayed at the shop, but he never thought they'd be anything other than normal incoming deliveries. Some of those nights, George had been here to intercept the shipments, but not always. His drivers had their own keys to the place. Alex now understands the mystery behind the Confederate flag bumper sticker, and the quiet dislike of David.

"Would I be lying if I told you I didn't wanna kill every damn negro who lives in this city?" George asks. "Yes. But I know I'm doing my share. I know exactly what's happening with the guns I'm delivering. I keep my own records." He points to the wall of photographs and newspaper clippings. "So I can live here, and I can raise my daughter without exposing her to any of this because deep down inside," he taps on his chest, "I know I'm honoring Clive and Alice. I know I'm doing right by them."

He sits back down in his chair and drops his face into his hands. His body trembles as he sobs. Alex takes a step toward him, but stops. He's not sure what to do. He's never seen a grown man cry before. He just watches until George straightens himself back up in his chair and wipes at his eyes and nose.

"Damn black bastard's got my little girl," he says. "I should've told her about Clive and Alice. I should've warned her about those people. When we first moved up here, there weren't any. Not a one. I figured she'd be safe even with the few who eventually came here. Not enough to do any damage, right?" He looks at Alex. "Not an easy thing to keep this all up inside, kid."

Alex nods. "I promise I won't tell anybody, Mr, McKnight."

George lets out a short, stifled laugh and grins. "I know you won't, Alex." He stands up and puts his hands on Alex's shoulders. "I'm sorry I put you through this. I shouldn't have asked you to spy on Sarah. I just…I guess I just see myself in you. I know what you've gone through. I've been there. And I know you love Sarah. I've known since I first asked you to come work for me."

Alex drops his head.

"No reason to be ashamed of it," George says. "Just wish I'd done more to stop this mess. Would give anything to get rid of that son-of-a-bitch."

He pulls Alex into his chest and hugs him. George's arms are thick and strong. At first, Alex keeps his own arms at his sides, but as his chest burns, his eyes stinging with tears, he lifts his arms and wraps them around George's waist.

"I love you, Mr. McKnight," he says.

George squeezes him. "I love you too, kid."

~

Alex lies on his back on top of his sleeping bag, the Glock gripped between his hands and pointed toward the ceiling. He's not comfortable pulling the trigger while in this position, so he makes a shooting noise with his mouth instead. The door leading to the shop is open, allowing a rectangle of fading afternoon light to trickle into the small room and illuminate the opposite end of it. One edge of the rectangle is cutting across the foot of the cot and the other is just to the left of the door now closed against George's secret office. Alex props himself up on his elbows and watches as the light slowly slips off the end of the cot, leaving his entire body covered in darkness as though he's just been swallowed by some kind of black hole. Gone. Dead.

The door to George's office is closed, the padlock once again dangling from the latch, secured tight and locked. The secrets revealed to Alex within the walls of that room are secrets he'll never share with anybody, ever. George confided in him and nobody else, not even his own daughter, the most important person in his world. And George expressed his love for Alex, and his desire to get rid of David. What did it all mean?

"Just wish I'd done more to stop this mess. Would give anything to get rid of that son-of-a-bitch."

The words drift in and out of Alex's mind. He drops his head back down onto his pillow and lifts the gun again, the nose of it pointed toward the ceiling.

"Bang," he whispers. "You're dead."

~9~

I pick a circle of pepperoni off the slice of pizza on my plate and put it on my tongue. It's spicy at first, but after a few seconds, it turns sweet. I swallow what remains of the pepperoni, and then eat a second small circle of meat. When we ordered the pizza, I thought I was hungry, but when the waitress placed it on our table, the smell of melted cheese and hot tomato sauce made my stomach turn. I hoped for the same reaction I had the other night when Dad brought pizza home for dinner, but it didn't happen.

"You need to eat, Sarah," Megan says.

We're sitting across from each other in a booth at Little Charlie's, a local pizza parlor known for its extra thin, melt-in-your mouth crust. On Friday and Saturday nights, Little Charlie's is the favorite place to hang for Kalispell High students, but on Sunday afternoons, it's quiet. Only one other booth is currently occupied—a young couple and their two small children—and two men are sitting at the bar watching ESPN Sports Center on one of the restaurant's three big-screen television sets.

"I know," I say. "I'm just not hungry."

"But you're okay, right? I mean, you said his parents were cool."

"Yeah, they were great. David had pretty much filled them in by the time I got there, so it was easy. They said it's our problem to take care of, and that we're adults, and no matter what we do, they'll support us."

"Sounds like something my parents would say."

Steve and Jennifer Cochran would definitely tie for first place with Clarence and Yvette Brooks in a "Coolest Parents on the Planet" contest. The amount of time David and I have hung out together as a couple at Megan's, with her parents, is about equal to how much time we've spent at David's.

"You sure you don't want me to come with you guys tomorrow?" Megan asks. She takes a bite from her slice of pizza.

"No," I reply. "Besides, you need to cover for me. With both of us gone, I'm sure there'll be rumors to squash."

Even though we've done our best to keep our relationship a secret, sometimes I feel like people would have to be completely stupid not to know there's something going on. But I also think the mere idea of a white girl and a black boy being anything more than just friends in this town is so beyond most people's comprehension, they won't allow themselves to believe it. I know with both David and me out of school tomorrow, somebody will think something, but when we both come back on Tuesday, nothing will be said.

Megan finishes her pizza and grabs another slice. We've been frequent Sunday afternoon visitors to Little Charlie's since last August. On Friday and Saturday nights, we always come with the whole group, so finding a chance to just sit and talk to Megan alone is difficult. On the Sunday after the first time David and I kissed at

Julie Allen's party, I sent Megan a text message asking if she could meet me here. It just seemed like the perfect place to tell her about David. Of course, she already knew.

"It's been completely obvious for months, Sarah," she'd said. "I was just waiting for you to tell me yourself."

From that day forward, we tried to meet on as many Sunday afternoons as we could. Just last weekend, we'd been here, laughing and talking about the same things we'd been laughing and talking about for months—who was seen making out with who at what party, or who got in trouble in which teacher's class for doing something ridiculously stupid, or who said what about who. All the normal "stuff" best friends might discuss on a lazy Sunday afternoon in the middle of spring. And after that last meeting, I went to David's house, and we locked ourselves in his bedroom where we made out like crazy in between 15-minute study sessions.

Today is different. And next Sunday will be different, and the Sunday after that will also be different. I don't care anymore about the latest kissing gossip or class clown stories or the backstabbing antics of our classmates. All I can think about now is getting through the next few days, and after that, I just don't know. I'm scared and sad and angry, and the combination of these emotions makes me tired. Maybe I'll feel the same way after the abortion. I just don't know. But what I *do* know for sure is my Sunday afternoons with Megan at Little Charlie's will never be the same, and that fact makes my heart ache.

"When this is all over," I say, blinking back tears, "we should all start coming here together on Sundays."

I can tell by the look on Megan's face she thinks I'm crazy. She leans back in her booth. "You sure about that? I mean, it's not like we don't all hang out together all the time anyways, but—"

"When have we all been together when there isn't a million other people around?"

She hesitates. "Never."

For as long as we've all been friends, we've never gone out in public alone, just the seven of us. At school and on the weekends, whether at parties or games or at Little Charlie's, we're always surrounded by classmates. For anyone standing on the outside looking in, nothing appears unusual because it's common knowledge that a couple of black kids attend Kalispell High.

"I think we should change that," I say.

I'm not sure if it's because I'm tired and nauseous or scared and sad and confused, but I'm suddenly sick of hiding and pretending, of constantly walking on egg shells, of being nervous about anybody who looks at me funny, like they might know I'm in love with an African-American. I wish I didn't have to keep a calendar where I crossed off each passing day with a permanent marker until the middle of August when David and I plan to leave. Only then, will I no longer be afraid of who might see us together.

"I think that's a great idea," Megan says.

"Me too." I eat another slice of pepperoni, but it no longer tastes like pepperoni, and I have to wash it down with water.

"Can we swing by Safeway before you drop me off?" I ask.

"Of course," Megan replies. "What's up?"

"Dad and I are having banana splits tonight."

She wipes her hands and mouth with a paper napkin. Not looking at me, she says, "What would he do if he found out?"

I drop my elbows onto the table and fold my fingers together. "I don't know, actually. It's really hard not being able to talk to him about this, but I know I can't. I used to imagine having a boyfriend who'd come over and hang out with Dad, and when I had kids someday, he'd be the best grandpa in the world. I never wanted to keep anything from him, especially something like this."

Megan sets her napkin on the table and leans forward. "Your dad has his own secrets, Sarah. You know there's more to this Clive

Sanders guy than what he's told you. He's never actually said what the guy did for him or why."

"My grandfather was abusive, Meg. I don't expect Dad to want to talk about it."

"But what about that picture you found when you were little of him and his sister? You said yourself he never talked about her again after that. He's obviously carrying around some baggage of his own he doesn't want to talk to you about. What we don't know, can't hurt us. This is no different."

I stare at my fingers, knowing she's right. I've never pried Dad on anything about his past, about my mother. Throughout my life, he's told me what he felt he needed to tell me, and I realize that. The picture of his sister, the bumper sticker, the words he mumbles under his breath when he sees President Obama on the television set. He loves me and he takes care of me, and that's all that's ever mattered.

"I don't think your dad just woke up one day and decided to hate black people," Megan says. "But whatever made him that way, he has his reasons for keeping it from you. Maybe because he's a single dad, I don't know, but it's good that he did. He's not a bad person, Sarah. It's not like he's running around killing people. He's never sold a gun to anyone and had it show up on the evening news. You and David just need to get to California. Maybe once you're there, you can tell your dad about him. What's the worst he can do?"

I look at her. "You're kidding, right?"

She shrugs.

"He owns a gun shop, Meg."

"Oh…right."

We both laugh, the first time in days.

~

I'm sitting at the dining room table, staring at the cartons of French vanilla and strawberry ice cream, the jar of hot fudge and the bag of honey-roasted peanuts. I'd sliced a whole banana in half and put the halves in two separate bowls, then set them on the table as well. When Dad comes home, we'll scoop our ice cream on top of the sliced bananas, and then top the bananas with too much hot fudge and a good quarter cup of peanuts each. After eating just six small slices of pepperoni at Little Charlie's, I'm starving. Hot fudge banana splits sound awesome right now, especially since all week the foods I've craved the most have been sweet, like Skittles and lemonade and cherries.

I glance at the wall clock behind me, the one I made in 7th grade industrial arts. It's a sanded-down, acrylic-coated piece of a tree trunk, an inch thick and about the diameter of a basketball. The cheap plastic Roman numerals I had to individually place on top of the wet acrylic are slightly crooked, but the clock was a Christmas present for Dad, and when I gave it to him, his eyes glossed over with tears. He kept every piece of artwork I ever made. Hanging on the far wall in the kitchen is the needlepoint framed in Popsicle sticks I made in 3rd grade. In the living room above the fireplace hangs the watercolor of a fruit bowl I painted in 8th grade (Dad had it professionally framed), and resting on the coffee table between the sofa and the television is the trinket basket I weaved from straw in my 10th grade art class. Even the centerpiece on the dining room table is a mess of plastic flowers stuck in floral Styrofoam inside of a hand-painted flowerpot I made in 2nd grade. It doesn't matter how ugly the stuff is, Dad has it all displayed, as though they're the most beautiful pieces of artwork in the world.

I look back at the cartons of ice cream, the containers sweating.

"He's obviously carrying around some baggage of his own he doesn't want to talk to you about. What we don't know, can't hurt

us...whatever made him that way, he has his reasons for keeping it from you."

"What're you keeping from me, Dad?"

The small hand on my industrial arts clock points to the Roman numeral seven, the big hand between the five and six. There are no missed phone calls on my cell phone, no text messages, no voicemail. It's not like him not to let me know where he's at, especially on a Sunday evening. He'd spoken to Alex Mackey on the phone this morning. I can only hope Alex is okay.

I rise from my chair and grab the two cartons of ice cream. I'll put them back in the freezer until Dad gets home. As I turn toward the kitchen, I hear the truck pull into the driveway. The blinds covering the living room window are closed, so I can't see it, but I know the sound of the Chevy's engine. I exhale a sigh of relief and put the ice cream back on the table.

I sit back down for five minutes, watching the front door and waiting for Dad to come bounding in. I want to see him smile when he catches his first glimpse of the ice cream and fudge and peanuts, the small bowls carefully crafted with sliced bananas. But another minute passes, and he still hasn't come inside.

I walk into the living room and peek through the blinds. Dad is sitting in his truck, his head down, his lips moving as though he's talking to a tiny person perched on his lap. He covers his face with his hands, wipes at both of his eyes, then steps from the truck and walks toward the front door.

I release the blind and move back to the table, wanting to believe Dad's behavior is because of what happened with Alex, but my rapidly beating heart knows better. The phone call he received this morning wasn't from Alex. It was from the person who'd been spying on David and me last night.

As the front door opens, I remain standing. Dad steps into the house and closes the door behind him. When he looks up, I see that his eyes are red and swollen. He fumbles with his keys, glancing back and forth between his hands and the door, as though he's considering whether to turn back around and leave.

"Dad?" I say.

He looks up again and meets my gaze. For a second, his eyes fall on the ice cream cartons resting on the table behind me. The smile I'd hoped to see is a frown instead. Not the pretend sad look he's given me the few times in the past when I'd actually broken a date with him to hang with my friends, but the sad look I've seen just one other time in my life—on the night I showed him the photograph of he and Alice.

He stares at his hands, his fingers tapping nervously against his keys. "I thought I was doing everything right by you. Didn't want you to see what I'd seen. Didn't want you to have to live like I lived."

My hands are shaking. I reach back with both and grip the edge of the dining room table.

"I never told you much about my life before you were born because it had nothing to do with you," he says, "and I figured we were so far away from Alabama, so far away from all that shit, I wouldn't ever have to worry about you getting mixed up with those kinds of people. I just wanted to be a good father. I wanted people to see that I was a good father."

Tears pool in my eyes.

"I can't be angry at you, Sarah," he says, his voice cracking. "I wanna be, but I can't. It's my fault this happened. My fault for not doing more for you, for thinking it best to keep my own experiences to myself and hope you'd figure the world out on your own. But I should've been guiding you. I should've been showing you the truth, showing what those people are."

My chest burns. I want him to scream at me. I want him to run toward me and raise his fist and hit me, strike me down and kick me, yell at me for being dishonest with him, for taking advantage of him, for not giving him everything like he's given me. But he doesn't. He stands still, his eyes on his hands, his keys clinking together as he flips them around with his fingers.

He looks at me. "I'm going to bed."

He walks up the stairs and disappears into his bedroom. I hear the click of the door closing behind him. My legs are trembling. I drop into the chair at the end of the table. The condensation from the ice cream cartons has made small puddles around the base of each. I put the tip of my finger into one of the puddles and drag the water toward me. The smell of the bananas makes me nauseas, so I throw them away and set the bowls in the sink, then stare at the ice cream and hot fudge and peanuts, the pain in my chest so heavy I think my lungs might actually collapse. I sit back down and sob, tears and snot dripping off my face and into my lap, my hands like lead on my thighs. My body is numb.

I don't know what else to do but cry, like somehow the more tears I shed, the less pain I'll feel in my heart. It seems like an hour has passed before I finally get up and toss the ice cream cartons into the trash on top of the bananas. I throw in the jar of hot fudge and the bag of peanuts, then look at the mess that was supposed to be our Banana Split Sunday. There won't be anymore, and I know it. And it's all my fault. How could I be so stupid? How could I be so selfish? I didn't have to be with David. I didn't have to fall in love with him. I knew what the consequences would be, what it would do to Dad if he found out, but I did it anyway. I let myself forget everything he's done for me, how much he's sacrificed to give me a good life, and I acted on my stupid, adolescent emotions. But I'll make it right. It's not too late. I'll get the abortion tomorrow, and then I'll end it. I'll tell David we can't be together.

I walk up the stairs and stop at the landing. There's no sound coming from Dad's bedroom, but the light is on. On Saturday mornings when I was little, I used to crawl into bed with him and lay my head in the crook of his shoulder. He'd flip the channel on the television from a hunting show or car racing or home remodeling program to my choice of cartoon, and we'd watch together, sometimes for hours. He never complained, never turned back to what he really wanted to see, never left me there alone while he went on with his day. When I was ready to get up, he'd get up.

I'm so sorry, Daddy.

I walk into my own bedroom and close the door, then lay on my back on top of my bed. My head hurts, my stomach is sour, and my throat is dry, but I don't care. The last of the day's light pushes past my open blinds and paints fire orange stripes across my closet door. On the shelf Dad installed a few feet below the ceiling is my collection of skiing and soccer trophies, lined up in order of receipt. I wanted to play soccer. I wanted to ski. And if it hadn't been for Dad, I wouldn't have been able to do either.

My cell phone vibrates against my hip. I pull it from my pocket and stare at the text message on the screen. It's from David.

I love you, Sarah.

I roll over and cry into my pillow.

~10~

Alex stands in front of the entrance to the Maple Leaf Mobile Park. At 11 o'clock and with nothing but a sliver of a moon in the sky, the world is dark. The hazy yellow light pouring from street lamps made his walk from the shop to the park possible, but the street lamps ended on the block behind him. Now, the only light visible is coming from the windows of the two or three trailers in the park where people are still awake, including his own.

He touches the handle of the Glock through his windbreaker. The gun is tucked between his jeans and his stomach. After George left the shop earlier, Alex walked through to see the damage caused by his outburst. All of the glass from the frames holding the Montana photos were broken, and four of the frames had been pulled off the wall and were lying face down in piles of splintered wood and busted glass. Two of the clothing racks that held hunting apparel had been knocked over, the shirts and jackets strewn across the floor like lifeless bodies. And the glass display case closest to the cash register was shattered. Before George left, he removed the guns from that case and locked them in another. He said he'd be in early tomorrow morning to clean up the mess and rearrange the cabinets until he could get the case repaired.

Alex had walked behind the busted display case. The Glock George took for the shooting range was normally stored there, but in the chaos of the prior 36 hours, he'd not asked for the gun back. Or, he didn't feel the need to. He'd wanted Alex to practice dry shooting. Even when he was trying to re-secure the guns from the damaged display case, he'd not asked for the Glock to be returned, and the ammunition for that gun was readily available in the little wooden drawers beneath the case. George was not able to lock the ammunition drawers, so to prevent the possibility of an accident, all of the guns were kept unloaded and securely locked up, and the alarm system in the shop was comparable to that of a bank. In the 17 years since George opened the shop, there'd never been an accident nor a robbery.

A cool breeze blows across Alex's face. He tucks his hands into the pockets of his windbreaker. The leaves in the two maple trees standing like statues on each side of the entrance to the trailer park come alive in the wind, the sound like a hundred whispering voices. As Alex crosses into the park, he looks up at the swaying branches of the trees, the stars in the sky blinking at him through the spaces between the moving leaves. When he reaches the concrete landing at the front door of his trailer, he stops and holds his breath. He hears muffled voices, laughter, then more voices. The sounds are coming from the television.

He steps onto the landing and inserts his key into the keyhole in the doorknob. This time, it's locked. He pushes the door inward a few inches, then stops and waits, expecting his father to grab the door and yank it open. But he doesn't. When Alex walks into the tiny living room, he sees his father passed out on the sofa wearing nothing but pajama bottoms. There are only three empty beer cans on the coffee table this time, but there are two full ashtrays instead of one, the second so overstuffed that several of the butts and a small smudge of ash litter the table. The room is only partially lit by the fluorescent kitchen light and the strobe-like flashes from the television. The short hallway that leads to both Alex's room and his parents is shrouded in darkness.

Alex steps closer to his father and peers down the hallway. Both bedroom doors are closed, and the space beneath his parent's door is black. His mother must be sleeping. The sickening, stale odor of pee fills his nose, and he wonders if his father got so drunk he pissed himself.

"Pig," Alex whispers.

He looks down at his father's face, thick salt-and-pepper stubble spread across his cheeks and chin like some kind of disease. His breath reeks of warm beer and cigarettes. Alex touches the gun again. He doesn't know why he's here. On the walk from the shop, the gun pressed against his lower abdomen, he thought he'd sneak in and grab his things—some clothes, his cell phone charger (he'd been using a spare one of George's), some books, his Portable Play-Station. He'd brought the gun along, just in case, and although he'd taken a magazine full of cartridges from one of the boxes of ammunition in the drawer, he hadn't loaded the weapon. He'd sat on the cot, the magazine in one hand, the Glock in the other. When he tried to slip the magazine into the gun, his fingers trembled and beads of sweat popped up across his forehead like unruly pimples. He pushed the magazine under his pillow and left with just the gun.

Alex's father snorts. His left arm rises above his protruding belly and into the air as though saluting someone. Then, just as quickly, it falls down, but rather than dropping back onto his stomach, it crashes into the coffee table, shooting the empty beer cans in three different directions. He sits up and grumbles.

"Christ, son-of-a-bitch," he says. He cradles his left arm against his chest.

Alex takes a short step back, and as he does, his father turns toward him, his eyes focused on Alex's feet. Then, slowly, he lifts his head to meet Alex's gaze. At first, Alex thinks his father might not recognize him. If he's drunk enough, he might not even identify him as anything other than a shadow. As his father stands shakily to his feet, however, Alex knows he's aware of his presence.

"Where the fuck you been?" he slurs.

Alex takes another reverse step, bumping into the bar stool behind him. In front of the bar stool is the portion of the kitchen counter that juts into the living room.. There's only one way for him to move now, and that's toward his father who's taken a step in his direction.

Alex straightens his back. His hands are shaking, but he doesn't move. He needs to stay where he is. His father will come to him, and when he does...

"I'm talkin' to you, boy," his father says. "You got your mother worried sick."

Alex opens his mouth to speak, but closes it again and clears his throat instead. His head is pounding, his heart racing. His skin prickles with gooseflesh. His father's eyes appear swollen in the milky glow of the kitchen light. The skin on his neck sags like a wet towel, and his chest droops like the breasts on an old lady. Alex thinks about his father's fists, rising and falling against his back and chest and stomach, deliberately striking him in places others won't see. He feels those fists, like rock hammers, pounding and pounding and pounding. He sees the blood from his mother's nose, tears pouring from her tired eyes, and the fear seems to slip away, anger swallowing it like a stormy sea to a boat.

"You listenin' to me?" his father hisses.

Alex slides his right hand beneath his windbreaker and wraps his fingers around the Glock's warm handle.

"No," he replies. "I'm not listening to you." His heart feels like it's going to explode.

His father places his hands on his hips. "What did say to me?"

"I said, I'm not listening to you." Alex tightens his grip on the gun's handle and pulls it slowly from his jeans. He holds it against his stomach, still hidden from sight under his windbreaker.

His father looks down. "What the hell you got there, boy?" He takes two steps toward him and stops.

Alex yanks the gun from beneath his jacket, and with both hands firmly gripping the handle, points the weapon at his father's face.

"You see it now?" he asks, his hands shaking.

The rosy red alcoholic glow in his father's cheeks fades to a pale splotchy pink. He stands with his arms at his sides, his saggy chin and neck quivering like a rooster's wattle. His dark eyes remain fixed on the end of the gun.

"Gonna hit me now, Dad?" Alex asks.

His father doesn't move. Alex hears the squeak of rusted hinges from down the hall. His mother steps into the dim light at the edge of the living room, her graying hair pulled back in a bun, her faded blue nightgown hanging lose over her frail body. She rubs at her eyes. When she looks up and sees the gun, she covers her mouth with one hand and leans back against the wall.

"Go ahead, you little punk," Alex's father says. "Pull the fuckin' trigger. You'll go to the state penitentiary and rot. Your mother'll be left all alone. You want that?"

From the corner of his eye, Alex sees his mother crying. "At least I'd know she'd be safe from you."

"Don't, Alex," his mothers says. "Don't do this."

Without looking at her, he replies, "Why do you stick up for his lazy ass? All he does is drink and hit you. Hit me. Why the fuck do you let him do that?"

She lowers her gaze to her feet, her head shaking as she sobs.

"You don't have to live like this, Mom," Alex says. His father remains still, but his shoulders begin to droop and his stomach slips and hangs like bread dough over the lip of his pajama bottoms.

"Get out of this house," he says. "Get your shit and get out."

With the gun still pointed at his father, Alex looks at his mother. Both of her hands are covering her face and her head is tilted at a 90 degree angle as though she's about to tumble forward onto the ground. Her knees are bent and shaking. Alex thinks if she was a dog, she'd have her tail tucked so far up between her legs he'd have to use a crowbar to yank it back out. He hates her for it, hates her for being so weak. He wants to give her the gun. He wants to show her how to use it. Maybe then, she wouldn't be so pathetic. Maybe then, she'd have the courage to walk away from this shithole and the sad and lonely life she lives with a man who smells like a sewer and punches like a boxer in training.

"Come with me, Mom," Alex says. He doesn't know where they'd go, but it's his last ditch effort to help her, like he'd tried so many times before.

"Get out!" his father shouts.

Alex looks back at him. He wishes now he'd had the strength to slip the magazine into the gun. He'd only considered scaring his father a little. He just wanted to see the look of panic in his face, smell the pungent odor of sweat with the rise of fear in the bastard's chest. But now, Alex wants to pull the trigger. He wants to put a bullet in his father's head and watch the life spill out of him, onto the dirty orange carpet alongside years of old beer and whiskey and crushed cigarette ash.

"I hate you," Alex says.

He keeps the gun pointed at his father as he walks between the sofa and the coffee table. Once in his bedroom, he stuffs some clothes, his cell phone charger, and his PSP into a small duffle bag from his closet. While he's packing, he keeps the gun aimed at the open door. Neither of his parents are there to watch, and for a split second, his chest hurts. He chokes back the rising lump in his throat, the stinging tears that bite at his eyes.

He tucks the gun into his jeans and walks back into the living room. His mother is now sitting on the floor, her knees pulled to her chest, her arms wrapped around her legs. She stares blankly at the edge of the coffee table in front of her. Alex's father hasn't moved from his spot, but as Alex walks behind him toward the front door, he turns to watch him leave.

"Don't you ever come back here," he says.

As Alex steps out of the trailer and onto the cement landing, he replies, "I'd rather die."

He doesn't turn back around as he passes between the two maple trees, their branches no longer swaying. The wind is gone, leaving the mobile park quiet and still. He wonders where it went. He used to believe wind traveled, and he'd wish to could go with it, see what it saw, touch what it touched—places far away from the Maple Leaf Mobile Park and Kalispell. Alex has never been anywhere else. As he crosses the street, he knows he'll never step foot inside the park again.

He stops in front of George and Sarah's house. The windows are dark. He doesn't know what happened after George left the shop. Did he go home? Did they argue? Did he tell Sarah the truth about his past, about the guns and the KKK? Did Sarah confess her pregnancy to him? Alex puffs out his chest, realizing he knows both of their secrets. And this knowledge is all that matters to him now. The joke that is his life finally has some meaning, some purpose. Why else would he have been standing against the wall of the high school right when Sarah and David walked out? He was meant to be there.

Alex turns and continues walking toward the gun shop. He used to wonder why his father beat him, why his mother stopped loving him. He used to blame himself. But if not for this, George never would've had a reason to help him. Their paths may never have crossed. Alex is here now because he is supposed to help George. It's why he didn't load the Glock earlier. If he had, he might've killed his father, and his real purpose, the meaning for his life, would not have been fulfilled.

Back at the shop, he sits at the edge of the cot. He holds the gun in his hands. He thinks about the small plaque hanging next to the window above the sink in his kitchen. His mother brought it home from a garage sale when Alex was eight years old, long before she stopped talking to him. It reads, *If You're Alive, There's a Purpose to Your Life*. Alex's father always made jokes about the plaque.

"Your purpose is to take care of me," he'd say to Alex's mother, and she'd nod her head in agreement.

Alex saw the words everyday, but they meant nothing to him. He thought maybe he'd discover his purpose later, but when he tried to imagine life beyond high school, his mind went blank, like the empty pages of a book that would never be finished. Now, it makes sense to him why he saw nothing but darkness. There is no life for Alex beyond now, and as he cradles the Glock in his hands, he thinks about Sarah and about the fleeting moment in 5th grade when he thought she cared about him. Truthfully, she didn't, and she never will. He used to believe he and Sarah could have a life together someday, but that's not true either. And when he completes the task, when he fulfills his life's purpose, she will hate him. And that's okay.

Alex reaches under his pillow and retrieves the magazine. He inserts it into the gun and pushes on the magazine until he hears the familiar click of it locking in place. He grips the frame of the Glock and pulls it backward, hearing another click, then releases the frame to its original position. He reaches beneath the cot and grabs the case for the gun. Carefully, he sets the weapon in the case, closes the lid, and slides the case back underneath the cot.

He lies on his back, his hands tucked behind his head, his eyes fighting to stay open. He's exhausted. He can't remember the last time he was this tired. But he also can't remember the last time he actually looked forward to another day. George had made life easier for him since offering him a job at the shop, but it didn't change how Alex felt on a day-to-day basis. There were lots of times when he considered killing himself. Once, he'd even made a noose from a stretch of rope he found in the front yard of a house not far from the mobile park. He tied the rope to the clothes rod in his closet and slipped it over his head. For a few seconds, he let himself hang there with his knees bent and his feet loose against the floor, but as the rope tightened around his throat, he realized the process would be too slow and painful, so he stood up and threw the rope away. He also knew if he committed suicide, it wouldn't matter. Nobody would care he was gone. There'd be some kind of assembly at the school, the hallways would buzz for a bit, his parents would receive some temporary sympathy from the community, but within weeks, maybe even days, the story would pass, and Alex would become just another statistic.

He doesn't want to become just another statistic. Tomorrow, he'll go to school and map out a plan. And on Tuesday, he'll fulfill his purpose.

~11~

When I walk out of my bedroom at 6:15 the following morning, I see that Dad's bedroom door is still closed. The house is cold and dark. There's no scent of fresh-brewed coffee in the air, no sound of Dad whistling in the kitchen or the familiar squeak of the utensil drawer being opened and closed. The living room blinds are shut, the small chandelier above the dining room table is off, and there's a stillness that reminds me of the mortuary my 9th grade biology class visited on a field trip. It's heavy, deep, quiet, and for a second, I hold my breath, just as we all did when we stepped into that bright empty morgue.

I place my hands flat against Dad's bedroom door and press my ear to the cold wood, but there's no sound. I think about knocking, but don't. I shower and dress, then walk into the kitchen, but the thought of eating anything makes me want to puke. I drink a glass of water instead and sit on the sofa, my hands folded in my lap. I can't remember the last time I felt this alone. Maybe never. When I was old enough to understand, Dad told me about my mother. I knew I was supposed to be sad, but I wasn't. I didn't feel like I missed her. What was there to miss? I didn't even know her. And later, when I started to wonder about her while watching my friends with their own mothers, I thought about what it would be like to meet her. But as the years passed, I stopped wondering. She wasn't, and never would be, a part of my life.

For the first time ever, I want my mother. I want to talk to her. When she was pregnant with me, she wanted an abortion. I know why she did, but I don't know what she was feeling. Was she confused like me? Was she scared? Did she decide against it because she knew Dad would take care of me? Does she miss me? Has she ever wanted to talk to me?

At 7:30, I get a text message from Megan.

I'm outside.

I open the front door, but pause for a second to look back up the staircase for any sign Dad is up—the sound of running water maybe, or a glimpse of light escaping from beneath his bedroom door. Silence. Darkness. I step out into the crisp morning. It's no different than any other late April morning. The sun shines bright and strong in a sky as blue as a glacier lake where just a few white wisps of clouds still linger. Soon, they'll burn off. The air is cool and ripe with the scent of dew-covered grass and honeysuckle. I'm greeted by the voices of birds—larks and finches, warblers and nuthatches. I don't normally pay such close attention to the sights and sounds and smells, but this morning *is* different. In just a few short hours, I'll be at the abortion clinic in Missoula. A doctor will examine me. I'll know exactly how pregnant I am. And then, I'll take the first of two pills to end my pregnancy.

The symphony of clicks and flitters and whistles, soothing in comparison to the silence inside the house, helps to calm my nerves, but as I reach Megan's car, the shrill of a lone raven pierces the morning air and temporarily scatters the orchestra of song birds. I look up toward the top of the telephone pole across the street and see a mess of sleek black feathers. The bird is too far away for me to even guess what it might be looking at, but I think it might be staring at me, its beady little eyes burrowing into my skin, watching the life growing inside my body and knowing it will soon be dead.

Ravens symbolize death. Right?

"You didn't sleep at all did you?" Megan asks as I lower myself into the passenger seat.

"No," I reply.

The few scattered clumps of minutes I did sleep were spoiled with nightmares of dead babies piled in heaps in a long shallow grave. In a separate shallow grave were the bodies of black men, one on top of the other from infants to old people, and standing at the edge of both graves was Dad, a shovel gripped in his dirty hands, his face ashen gray.

I close my eyes. I need to tell Megan about last night, but I don't have the energy. I can't talk about how I have to end my relationship with David because of Dad's bigotry. She won't understand, even though it's not an uncommon problem in this predominantly white community. Clarence once told me that it was part of being black.

"Makes us work that much harder to prove we're more than just a stereotype," he'd said.

And both he and Yvette did just that. Yvette is the only African-American nurse at the hospital, and within months of her start at Kalispell Memorial, she was given the title of Head Nurse. Clarence is a real estate agent with an office in Whitefish and a client list that includes a number of big names in both entertainment and sports. It didn't happen overnight. He had to push through the invisible boundary placed on him by some people in the community, but once he did, he couldn't be stopped. And he did it through dedication and honesty and showing respect for everybody, even though he wasn't always met with the same level of decency.

That same sense of pride and a desire to show he's more than the color of his skin is just one of the reasons I love David so much. My heart aches, and it's a hurt I've never felt before—deep and suffocating like a metal jacket is locked around my chest and slowly crushing my lungs.

Oh, please.

"I can't breathe," I say. "Megan, I can't breathe."

She pulls to the curb, and I open the door and throw up.

"It's okay, sweety," she says as she rubs my back. "It's okay."

But it's not okay. I sit back in my seat and shut the door. "Just get me to David's house, Meg."

When we arrive, David is sitting in his car in the driveway. Megan pulls in behind him. As I get out, she grabs my wrist. "I love you, Sarah. I'll have my phone on vibrate and in my pocket all day. Call me if you need me."

I nod, then step away and watch her back out of driveway and disappear down the street. When I open the Camry door, David stares at me as I sit in the passenger seat, but I don't turn to meet his gaze. When he reaches across the console to take my hand, I cross my arms over my chest. The motion feels strange to me. We've never gotten into a fight before, but not letting him touch me makes me feel like that's exactly what we're doing. Fighting.

"Baby, please," he says. "Talk to me. You didn't respond to any of my text messages last night. I need to know you're okay. What's going on?"

He'd texted me three more times after the initial "I love you, Sarah", but I hadn't looked at any of them. I turned my phone off and put it in my school bag and hadn't retrieved it since.

"I just wanna get this over with," I say.

And once it's done, I'll tell David I can't see him anymore. I won't tell him about last night. I'll blame it on the pregnancy and the abortion. I'll blame it on him and his parents. They're the ones who said I should get an abortion. Why? Maybe deep down inside, they really don't want their son to be with a white girl. They don't want mixed grandkids. But even as I let the idea swirl around inside my head, I know it's not true. It's just an excuse to make it appear as though Dad's not to blame for this.

"Okay," David replies.

We follow the same route Megan and I took on Friday, through Bigfork to Polson where David turns left onto Highway 93. Missoula is about 70 miles south of Polson. We haven't spoken since we pulled out of his driveway. He tries twice to hold my hand, but I keep my fingers locked together and resting on my knees, my eyes straight ahead at the nearly empty span of highway. In late April, this stretch of 93 is only lightly dotted with morning traffic—some commuters to Missoula, but mostly ranch trucks and farm equipment, horse trailers and an occasional 18-wheeler.

I want more than anything to feel the warmth of David's skin on my hand. I crave it the way I used to crave my morning coffee before I started throwing up last Monday. Like that morning coffee, David holding my hand is natural to me, a simple part of my life that makes me smile. Without it, I'm weak. Tired. Unfulfilled. But skipping coffee was uncontrolled, a reaction to the way my stomach felt, a means to not making me even sicker than I was. Not letting David reach over and touch my skin is painful and unnatural, like placing my hand on a burning hot stove, and right now, I'd prefer the latter.

I turn and look out my window. I haven't been on this road since last summer when Megan and I drove down to Missoula with her brother to check out the University of Montana campus. She'll be starting classes there in September. Because both of her parents work at the community college in Kalispell, Megan's been guaranteed a nearly tuition-free education, but that's not the only reason why she's going to school there. Unlike me, Megan has no interest in leaving Montana, and because she wants to be a journalist, she couldn't find a better school for it than the U of M.

When we visited the campus last summer, we got there early in the morning and hiked Mount Sentinel to the Big M above the university. We bought burgers and ate on a blanket by the Clark Fork River in Caras Park. We stood in the chilly water up to our knees, and then joined a group of little kids on the carousel. That night, we snuck into a college bar with Chris and drank beers while he sipped soda. He'd promised to be the designated driver.

"I wish you'd go to school with me in Missoula," Megan had said on the drive home that night, just before passing out with her head resting on my shoulder.

I look at the Mission Mountains to the east, looming like familiar blue giants, their peaks still capped with snow. The valley below is wide and vast, green like sour-apple candy in some places and gold like butterscotch in others. I can't remember exactly when I decided I wanted to leave Montana. It seems everyone I care about came from a big city—Megan from Minneapolis, Emma from Seattle, David from Denver. Jalen's family moved here from Chicago, and Reggie came from Portland, Oregon. I've never been anywhere, never even seen a big city with my own eyes. Even Coop's family—long-time Montana ranchers—has done enough traveling to appreciate the complexities of different cultures. There's more to life than Kalispell—a small town with a large demographic of small-minded people. Even before I started dating David, Los Angeles appealed to me because of its size and diversity. And it's on the ocean. I've never been to the ocean. I became obsessed with the idea of moving to L.A., of going to school there, of living a city life. And then I met David, and it seemed like it was all meant to be.

But just because I want something different, doesn't necessarily mean it's right. I look at David sitting next to me. He's just like Los Angeles. Different. And maybe this was all supposed to happen because I'm not supposed to leave. I'm supposed to stay here and take care of Dad. I'm not supposed to go to L.A., and David and I aren't supposed to be together. I belong here, in Montana where Dad chose to take me and raise me, away from the mess that was his life.

We continue driving in silence until the Interstate 90 interchange. As David merges onto the freeway, he says, "You haven't said a word since we left Kalispell, Sarah. Please talk to me."

In the distance are Mount Sentinel and the Big M, but we'll be pulling off the freeway long before reaching the exits to downtown Missoula and the U of M campus.

"What do you want me to say?" I ask. "We'll talk when this is all over."

"Sure," David sighs.

He takes the Reserve Street Exit to West Broadway. After several miles, he turns right, and then a quick left into the parking lot of the women's clinic. He stops the car, temporarily blocking the entrance, and leans forward, his eyes wide and unflinching. I see them too—a small crowd of about ten—standing on the sidewalk in front of the building. I can't hear what they're saying, but I see the words written on the signs some of them carry.

ABORTION KILLS BABIES
ABORTION = MURDER
GOD IS PRO-LIFE

"Shit," David whispers.

My knees start shaking as I recall what Megan told me. Without realizing what I'm doing, I put my hand on David's arm.

"What should we do?" I ask.

He drives forward and pulls into an empty spot at the far edge of the parking lot, then kills the engine.

He turns to me. "We just have to act like they're not there." He puts his hand over mine, his skin warm, the feel of his fingers erasing the jumbled mess of thoughts from my head. I don't try to pull away this time. "I won't let anyone hurt you, Sarah. I never will."

This *is* where I belong. Right here, with David. His face turns fuzzy behind the tears in my eyes.

"You ready?" he asks.

I take a deep breath and nod. We step from the car, David moving slightly ahead of me, and approach the picketers. I keep my head down, not wanting to look into anyone's eyes, but I hear their voices.

"Don't kill your baby!" a woman shouts.

"God punishes murderers!" a man yells.

"Your baby has a right to live, just like you!"

"You'll burn in hell!"

As we draw closer to the crowd, David reaches back and takes my hand in his. He squeezes my fingers. The shouting suddenly stops, but in the murmur that follows, I hear a woman say, "sinful". The air is momentarily still, as though the picketers have vanished. But when I look up, I see they're still there, staring at us as we continue moving toward the front doors of the clinic. Several of them have turned around and are walking away. The signs are all lowered.

"Over here," one of the men who's retreating shouts to the rest of the group. "Don't bother with them."

At the opposite corner of the building, coming from a different area of the clinic's parking lot, is a young couple. They appear a little older than us, but not by much. College students, maybe. They're also holding hands and walking toward the building.

David continues moving, but I stop and grip his fingers. The picketers approach the other couple, their voices rising again, their signs popping back up into the air, but rather than turn away from the young couple the way they did to David and me, they try and step in front of them. They try and block the path leading to the front door of the building. The young man puts his arm around the woman and they quicken their pace, the picketers growing louder and more aggressive as they do. When the couple finally enters the building, the crowd retreats and gathers quietly at the opposite end of the sidewalk from where David and I are standing, as though we're not even there anymore. One woman, her wispy graying hair pulled back in a bun, turns and stares at us, but when I try to make eye contact with her, she looks away.

I feel the heat rising in my face, my hands shaking, the muscles in my back and neck tightening. David steps in front of me and wraps his fingers around my forearms.

"It's okay, Sarah," he says. "Don't let this bother you."

I look at his face, the light brown of his eyes, his full lips, his dark skin. He's not angry or sad or ashamed. There's no sense of embarrassment, no regret. This is everyday life for him.

Did you know he walked right by my dad on the street a few months ago, and he wouldn't even look him in the face. Just walked right by like my dad wasn't even there. Like he didn't exist.

For the first time since David and I started dating, I understand what it's like for him. For his mom and dad and little sister. For Jalen and Reggie. David and I have been hiding our relationship because we knew we wouldn't be accepted. But until now, the only people who really knew about us were our friends—people who've been *helping* us keep our secret.

One of picketers told the others not to bother with us. Why? Is my baby not good enough to be spared? Do they not see my baby as a gift, a soul worth saving, as they did the other woman who made it inside? I'm white. David is black. The other two were both white. I heard a woman say, "sinful", and I know she was referring to David and me. Does that mean our baby is 'sinful' too?

David is talking, but I can't hear his voice over the pounding in my head. I pull away from him and walk toward the crowd of picketers now standing around talking and laughing, pretending we aren't there.

"Sarah," David says as he grabs my arm. "Don't."

I turn to him, place my hand on his cheek, and kiss him, then free my arm and continue walking, leaving him standing alone near the front door of the building. The woman with the graying hair looks up, but before she can walk away, I step in front of her and grab the sign from her hand.

"Respect all life as a gift from God," I read. The woman is waving at the others. From the corner of my eye, I see someone walking toward us.

"Why don't you try and stop me like you did that other girl?" I ask her. "Isn't my baby a gift from God?"

She looks at the ground.

"I can't hear you," I say.

"What's going on, Deidre?" It's the man who told the rest of the group not to bother with us. His cheeks are red beneath the dirty bill of his baseball cap.

"It's okay for me to get an abortion because my boyfriend's black. Is that it?" I ask him.

He doesn't respond, his eyes focused on David as he walks up behind me.

"What? Now you can't talk?" I ask.

"Come on, Deidre," he says. He puts his arm over the woman's shoulder, the skin beneath her eyes sagging like a wet paper towel.

"And you call us sinful," I say.

They turn away and walk toward the rest of the group.

"Good job," I shout, loud enough for all of them to hear. "You saved a baby today. Mine!"

I watch them all look at each other, shrug their shoulders, whisper. Deidre doesn't turn back around.

David's hands are on my shoulders.

"Let's go home," I say.

~12~

Alex is sitting across from Dustin in the crowded senior cafeteria. Dustin is talking, but Alex doesn't hear any of the words spilling out of his mouth. Instead, he's replaying in his mind the steps he needs to take tomorrow—where he'll tuck the gun, when he'll pull it out and how, what he'll do after he shoots David. In order for his plan to work, he'll need to walk up to David as though he wants to talk to him, maybe to say thank you for helping him last Monday. But more importantly, he'll need to do something prior to this that will draw Joe Berger's attention—that will make Joe approach him while he's approaching David. The three of them need to be within an arm's reach from one another. And then Alex will need to make sure he hits David high—in the heart or neck or head. If he misses any of those spots, David could live, and Alex will have failed.

As he imagines the scene, a bubble of nervous energy builds in his stomach. He's not sure if it's excitement or anxiety, but the sensation sends a cool chill up the back of his neck. The sound of the gun will send a shock wave through the cafeteria. Chaos will erupt. Nothing like this has ever happened at Kalispell High, but Alex will need to remain calm. He'll need to sit down on the floor and cradle the gun and wait for the police to come and take him away.

Emma and Randy are sitting at the table by the wall of windows. Megan, Reggie and Jalen are there too, but Sarah and David are both gone. Alex takes a deep breath. Even though his fingers are clasped together and resting on his lap beneath the table, his hands are shaking. He's scared. Not the kind of scared he felt when he was little and thought monsters were living in his closet. And not the kind of scared he felt in 8th grade when a guard dog chased him and Dustin through the cemetery on the other side of town. This fear is deeper and stronger and more real than anything he's ever felt. It's the kind of fear he'd expect to feel if he'd just been told he has terminal cancer. There's a cloud of uncertainty that lingers with this fear—of death maybe, or a trip to the unknown with no return ticket. An end.

"You okay, dude?" Dustin asks. "You look like you're gonna puke or something. You're all…pale."

Alex straightens up. "Yeah. I'm good. I'm fine."

Dustin stares at him for a few seconds, and then starts up about he and Jason Maxwell getting high yesterday in the clock tower of the playground at the city park near his house. Alex is glad Dustin and Jason are friends. After tomorrow, Dustin won't have anybody else at the school. It's too bad Jason is a junior and has to eat in the other cafeteria. Dustin will be alone at lunch for the rest of the year. Alex feels bad about this. He feels bad that Dustin will probably be treated even worse after tomorrow because people will think he must've known something, no matter what Alex tells the police.

"It was my idea," he'll say. "Dustin had nothing to do with it. I stole the gun from the shop. I just wanted to scare Joe Berger, but… the gun went off accidentally…and…"

David will be dead, and Alex will go to prison for manslaughter for five or ten, maybe 20 years. People will remember him. Some will even honor him. He won't just be another statistic.

At the sound of the bell, Alex and Dustin get up from the table and place their trays on one of the racks near the cafeteria's kitchen. They share 5th period physics with Joe. During class, Joe flirts with Amy Lang, one of the varsity cheerleaders. Twice, Mr. Loeffler asks Joe to be quiet, but he continues to lean over and whisper in Amy's ear. When he turns and catches Alex watching him, he drops his hand below his desk and flips him off. Alex smiles, lowers his own hand, and returns the gesture. Joe's face turns red. Anger? Embarrassment? Alex isn't sure, but when Joe points his finger at him and mouths the words "you're dead", Alex gives him a wink, then turns toward the front of the classroom.

His heart is racing and his palms are damp, but he keeps his gaze on Mr. Loeffler. He has no doubt Joe will keep his promise. He won't kill Alex, but he'll beat the shit out of him. He's done it before to other people, after school and off campus to avoid suspension. Joe will wait in his car at the end of the street, and when Alex walks by on his way to the shop, Joe will jump him. It's a customary Joe move. Alex will show up tomorrow with a bruised face, and before the day even begins, Joe will have bragged enough to his buddies for the whole school to know what happened. And Alex will have his final reason for wanting to scare Joe Berger.

At the end of class, Alex hustles out of the room, leaving Dustin scrambling to catch up with him in the hallway. Even though Joe won't do anything until after school, Alex would rather not cross his path again until then. Fortunately, they don't share 6th period calculus or 7th period English together, and while Mrs. Keatley and Ms. Sharone conduct their separate lectures, Alex ponders whether he should get rid of Joe too. But this isn't about Alex. He won't stray from his life's purpose, and that purpose is to help George. Joe Berger Sr. is one of George's best customers and oldest friends, and killing the younger Joe would cause more harm to George than good, regardless of how exhilarating it might be for Alex.

Sure enough, at the end of the day as Alex is walking down the sidewalk, away from the school, he sees Joe's pick-up pulled to the curb at the bottom of the street. He's alone in the cab. When Alex reaches the end of the street, he turns left and starts walking toward town. He wants to run, wants to avoid the pain and humiliation of being beaten up by Joe, but he can't. He needs the bruises. He needs the anger.

Two blocks later, Joe drives up behind Alex and stops the truck a few car lengths ahead. He jumps from the cab, runs across the street, and punches Alex in the face. The blow sends lightening pain through his entire body. He stumbles backwards, but Joe grabs the front of his t-shirt and punches him two more times, then shoves him to the ground and kicks him once in the stomach, knocking the air out of his lungs and leaving him gasping for breath like a fish out of water.

"Might wanna think before you give me the bird again, Mackey," Joe says. He spits, then turns and runs back to his truck.

When Alex is finally able to breathe again without coughing, he removes his windbreaker and wipes the blood from his stinging nose. His right eye is beginning to swell. He stands and continues walking in the direction of the gun shop, not sure what he'll tell George when he gets there. Maybe he can sneak into the back bathroom and at least wash his face before George sees him.

But when Alex reaches the shop, he's surprised to find it closed. The lights are off, and broken glass and splintered wood still blanket the floor. If George had come in at all today, he would've at least swept up the damaged frames. Alex walks to the front of the shop and peers through the door. Stuck on the outside glass at eye level is a square yellow post-it note. The words on the paper were written on the sticky side so they could be read by whoever was inside the shop, rather than somebody standing outside.

George,
can't remember the last time you
weren't here for your Monday coffee.
Hope everything is okay.
Marge

Alex walks to the back of the shop and sets his backpack on the cot. He takes his cell phone from his bag and dials George's number, but it goes directly to voicemail. It's not like him to turn his phone off.

Maybe he's dead. Maybe he killed David and then himself, and Sarah witnessed the whole thing.

Alex hurries into the bathroom and rinses the blood from his face. He takes the bar of soap and scrubs away the stains on his windbreaker and the few splatters of red on his t-shirt. He considers grabbing the Glock, but decides against it. If he gets to George's house and he's dead, and the police are there, he can't have a gun on him.

On the walk to George's house, he keeps his head down and his hands tucked into the pockets of his windbreaker. He hopes he finds George alive and well. He loves him. But with each step, his concern fades. The heavy pounding in his chest slows, and a slight tension creeps into his neck and shoulders. His skin burns. If George did kill David and then himself, what's left for Alex to do? He's taken everything that's happened over the past week as a sure sign getting rid of David is his life's purpose. Alex stops. If George and David are both dead, Sarah's alone. She has no mother, no siblings, no cousins or aunts and uncles or grandparents. And Alex is alone.

He takes a step forward, and then another and another until he's nearly running, his heart once again beating rapidly, a smile spreading across his face as though he's just eaten the sweetest piece of candy in the world. He pulls his hands from his pockets and cups them over his mouth as he thinks about holding Sarah to his chest and comforting her—rub her back, whisper that she's going to be okay. Just like a boyfriend would. He imagines them living in her house, the two of them together where they belong. He always knew Sarah would eventually come back to him, somehow.

He looks up, realizing he's just a few blocks from Sarah's house, and stops. David's silver Camry is parked at the curb about ten yards ahead. Alex ducks behind the maple tree at the edge of the yard of the little white house on his left, but he keeps his eyes on David's car. He's too far away to identify the two people sitting in the Camry, but he isn't stupid. Unless it had been stolen, and whoever the perpetrator is just happened to park the damn thing two blocks from Sarah's house, the shadows in the car are David and Sarah.

Alex leans against the maple tree. He wants to fall to his knees and cry, but he remains pressed against the thick trunk, its bark cool and rough on the palms of his hands. He takes a deep breath and holds the air in his lungs, hoping it might push the pain out of his heart, but the heaviness remains when he blows the air back out. Further down the row of houses, Alex sees where George's truck would be parked in his driveway, but the space is empty. He's not home, and he didn't come to work. The ache in Alex's chest deepens. George must be dead, and Sarah and David are sitting like innocent lovers in David's car, like they've done nothing wrong, like their sickening behavior didn't drive George to possibly take his own life.

Alex walks out from behind the tree and watches through the rear window of the Camry as David and Sarah lean toward each other. Their shadowed figures merge into one massive head as they kiss. Alex counts the seconds—one, two, three…four…five. Time suddenly slows to a crawl, as though this moment isn't real, but rather a scene in a movie or a television show. He turns away from the distorted vision in the car and walks back the way he came, toward the empty dark shop, the shattered glass, the little yellow sticky note flapping in the wind against the door.

Back in his room, sitting on the cot, the Glock loaded and ready to go, Alex wonders if George felt any pain when he died. He tries calling him again, but the only voice he hears is George's pre-recorded message.

"Hi, you've reached George McKnight. I'm out and about and unable to get to my phone, so leave me a detailed message, and I'll be sure to get right back atchya when I can. Have a great day!"

Alex disconnects the line. There are no new text messages or voicemails on his phone. He searches the small room and then goes into the shop. He looks in the cash register, in the ammunition drawers, on the corkboard in the back where George lets people post information about gun shows or events. But there are no notes or messages from George.

As Alex sits back down on the cot, he thinks about Clive and Alice and the last 17 years of George's life, and he realizes George did leave him a message. He purposefully didn't ask for the Glock back because he knew Alex would use it, and he knew Alex had access to the ammunition drawers. The gun would be traced back to the shop, the secret room would be discovered, and George would spend the rest of his life in prison, fully aware that the most important person in the world to him, his reason for living and breathing, would never forgive him. He knew Sarah's hatred toward him for what he did would be as deep and would last as long as his hatred for the people who took Clive and Alice from him.

Alex lies back on the cot and tucks his hands behind his head. His life's purpose isn't to help George. It's to honor him in his death.

~13~

"I have a bad feeling about this, Sarah," David says. "I just do. I think you should run in and get some clothes and let me take you to Megan's house. You have plenty of time before he gets home." He glances at his watch. "It's almost 4:30. He closes the shop at five, right?"

We're parked two blocks from my house, but I can see Dad's truck is not in the driveway. I wish I hadn't said anything to David about what happened last night, about Dad knowing the truth. He was already a nervous wreck after what had happened at the clinic.

"We'll just come back another day," he'd said as we walked away from the picketers and back to the car. "They can't be here all the time. We'll bring Megan with us next time, and the two of you can go in together, and I can walk in by myself a little later. I can still be there with you."

I waited until we were back on Highway 93 heading north toward Kalispell before I told him I didn't want to get an abortion.

"You're just angry, Sarah," he'd said. "Let's take a few days and think about things."

"There's nothing to think about," I replied. "I'm not letting them win. Not them. Not my dad."

We didn't speak much the rest of the drive home.

David turns to me now. "I don't think you should stay here."

"He's not gonna hurt me," I say. "He barely said anything last night. He wasn't angry, David. He was...sad. I told you, he went to bed, and he was still in bed when I left the house. He's never done that."

"All the more reason for me to worry."

I reach across the console and place my hand on David's thigh. "I can't avoid him. I need to try and talk to him and make him understand. There are far too many secrets between us. I need to know why he hates you, and I need him to know why I love you, and I can't do that without confronting him."

David puts his hand over mine. "Is that what it'll take for you to go through with the abortion?"

I sit back in my seat and cross my arms over my chest. I think about the harsh silence at the clinic when David took my hand in his, our cue those people wanted me to terminate my pregnancy, wanted me to rid the world of my 'sinful', mixed-race baby. I know David and I can't keep it, but I also know I can't get an abortion now. Not after what happened. David and I are good people, and I want the world to know how much we love each other.

"Sarah," he says, "having this baby isn't going to prove anything. It's not gonna change the way people look at us, no matter where we live. This isn't about them or us. It's about you and me. It's about our future together. I don't want us to end up like my Aunt Sade. I've seen that picture."

"That's different, David."

"How? How is it different? She got pregnant at 16. She put off her plans of going to college. Anthony tried going to school and working a job. At 18, she had another kid and Anthony split. The only difference between them and us, Sarah, is that they're both black, and they didn't have the opportunities we have. Anthony didn't have a football scholarship. Sade isn't stupid, but she doesn't have your brains."

Why can't he see this the way I do?

"So this is about your football scholarship?" I say.

David grips the steering wheel with both hands. He squeezes it so hard his knuckles almost turn white. He takes a deep breath in, and as he releases the air from his lungs, his fingers loosen their chokehold on the steering wheel. The blood rushes back into his knuckles, returning his skin to its natural chocolate brown.

"This isn't about my football scholarship," he says. "I love you, Sarah, and I'm gonna marry you someday. But we need this time right now to find our place in this world, to make a good life, before we bring our children into it." He drops his hands from the steering wheel and turns to me. "We need a chance to be us first, out there in the real world, because our kids are always gonna be looked at differently, no matter what."

I look down at my stomach, my eyes burning with tears. "Didn't any of that mean anything to you? Those people wanted us to kill our baby."

"It means everything to me," David replies. "But my whole life is like that. For you, it was new and scary. You don't walk around everyday expecting people to treat you differently. I do. I don't wanna be different, Sarah. I wanna approach this like any other high school couple would who has a future to look forward to."

Tears slip from my eyes and drop onto my lap.

143

"I'm sad too, baby," he says. "You don't think I think about our child, about what it might be, what we'd name it? I haven't stopped thinking about it since Friday, but I know we can't do this right now. I don't want those people at the clinic to win anymore than you do, and as much as getting rid of me might please your dad, having this baby isn't showing any of them up. In the end, Sarah, they won't care either way, and we'll have changed the direction of our lives for no other reason than we were trying to make a statement."

He reaches over, places his hand on the back of my neck, and pulls me toward him. He kisses the top of my head. I don't want him to be right, but he is. For a brief moment, I'll feel like I've conquered the world, that I've shown every person out there who turns in disgust at David and me that we're better and stronger than them. But days will pass, then months, then years, and our life will be far from what we'd planned and hoped. And Dad will not have changed by it, and neither will the people at the clinic. They'll continue to hate because that's who they are.

"I had to find a smart guy," I say, wiping the tears from my eyes. "Of all the boys at our school, I had to find a smart one."

David smiles. "Dad always says it's my duty to be smart. I'm a young black man. I owe it to other young black men."

"I love you," I say. "I really love you."

He leans forward and places his lips on mine. They're warm, and salty from my tears. I touch his cheek, then slide my fingers down and across his neck before resting my hand on his shoulder. When I pull my lips away, I drop my head against his chest, my ear pressed to his shirt, and listen to his heart, the slow steady thumping like a lullaby. I'm tired. So tired.

"I still think you should stay with Megan tonight," David says.

All I want to do right now is sleep, my face snuggled against his chest, the warmth of his body seeping through his shirt and teasing my skin. Maybe tonight isn't the best night to talk to Dad. I lean forward and pull my cell phone from my school bag at my feet.

I type a text message to Megan, **Can I stay with you tonight?** It doesn't take long for her to respond.

Of course! Where are you? Been worried sick.

Long story. Getting some clothes. David will drop me off in a few.

K. I'm at the house. See you soon.

I kiss David. "I'll be right back."

"Hurry."

I step from his car and look down the length of the sidewalk in both directions. The brightness of the day is fading to a burnt orange with the rapidly setting sun. Long shadows from trees paint jagged rectangles of gray across the front yards of the houses along the two-block stretch between David's car and my house. When I finally reach the front door, I pause before inserting my key into the lock. I know Dad's not home, but my hands shake anyway. It's a bizarre feeling to be afraid to walk into my own house, as bizarre as not letting David touch my hand in the car earlier today.

The living room and kitchen are dark. The faint odor of stale coffee lingers in the air. Dad must've gotten up not long after I left.

"Dad?"

My voice returns to me in a shallow echo. I look up the staircase. His bedroom door is closed. I shut the front door and walk through the living room to the dining room table. On the table is a folded piece of notebook paper with my name scribbled across the top. My hands are shaking again. I pick up the piece of paper and unfold it.

Sarah,

I have to go away for awhile. I'm sorry. I can't talk to you or look at you right now. I know this is all my fault.

I didn't tell you about what happened to me because I wanted to protect you from it. It was already too much that you didn't have a mother. I thought when you were little I'd be able to talk to you when you got older, but I never did. You were always so happy, and we had a good thing going. Why would I want to spoil that? I thought it was better to keep my secrets to myself. But now I'm not so sure. I'm sorry, Sarah. I'm sorry I wasn't a better father, and I'm sorry for whatever happens now. I only hope you can forgive me someday.

Dad

I refold the letter and hold it to my chest. I wish I were a little girl again, playing soccer in the backyard with him, laughing as he grabs me by the waist and tickles me for kicking the ball between the two soda cans we used as goal posts. His tickles always hurt a little, but I loved it anyway, and I'd try extra hard to make another goal, and then another, just so I could laugh until I couldn't breathe. I used to think Dad's hands were made of steel, they were so thick and strong. On Saturday mornings when we'd watch cartoons together in his bed, I'd spread my fingers over his and gaze at the difference in their shape and size. His were smooth like the skin of a peach, and I'd giggle and call him "fruity fingers," and he'd grab me and soak my cheeks in slobbery kisses.

I open the letter and read his words again, unable to keep myself from crying, his voice only in my head now as I try to remember what he sounds like. He's never left me alone for more than a few hours, not once in 18 years. He doesn't have any friends outside of Kalispell, at least none that I know of. Where would he have gone?

"I'm sorry for whatever happens now," I read. "I only hope you can forgive me someday." I sit down at the table. "I don't understand, Daddy."

When my cell phone rings, I jump. It's David.

"Hello," I say.

"You're scaring me, baby. It can't take that long to grab some clothes."

I struggle to keep my voice from shaking. "I'm…fine. Just give me a few more minutes. He's not here, David. The house is empty."

"You're crying, Sarah. What's wrong?"

"He left…he left a note. He's gone. I'll be out in a minute."

I hang up and tuck the phone into the back pocket of my jeans. As I walk up the stairs, I look down into the living room. Slivers of late afternoon light poke through the thin spaces between the window blinds, creating a dusty transparent haze that floats like early morning fog above a lake. But it's not calming, like I'd expect to feel if I was standing at the edge of that lake. Instead, the hazy living room scares me, as though hidden within the floating dust cloud is something dark and hideous.

I run up the stairs and into my bedroom where I grab a clean shirt and jeans, a fresh pair of socks and underwear. In the bathroom, I put my toothbrush and make-up in my toiletry bag. I'll borrow everything else from Megan. Before I walk back downstairs, I stop in front of Dad's bedroom door. Even though I know he's not there, I hold my breath as I knock. I wrap my fingers around the doorknob and turn it, then push the door open.

His bed is made, his closet door is shut, and his dresser drawers are all closed. The framed photographs of he and I—one of us when I was six sitting on a display case at his shop with him standing behind me, and another of the two of us at a soccer match when I was in 8th grade—remain on top of the dresser. I walk into his bathroom. His toothbrush and toothpaste are resting next to the sink. I open the sliding mirror to reveal his hair tonic, his lotion, his cologne. Wherever he went, he didn't think he needed these things. I go back into his bedroom and open his dresser drawers, then his closet. There doesn't appear to be anything missing, but that doesn't mean he left without a few changes of clothes.

Does it?

I sit at the edge of his bed, my eyes fixed on the two framed photos on his dresser, and I suddenly realize I don't know this man. I've never really known him. And by not knowing him—not knowing the story of Alice or Clive Sanders—I don't really know myself. And I have nobody to talk to about it, nobody to go to with questions. I used to think it didn't matter. Dad and I were just fine on our own. There'd never be a reason for me to wonder. But I was wrong.

I hug my clothes and toiletry bag to my chest. I feel hollow, like I'm nothing but skin wrapped around emptiness, and that emptiness is deep except for the life that's growing inside me. Like me, it has no idea who it is. And like Dad, its entire existence is a secret, a growing mass of unknown.

My cell phone rings from inside my back pocket. It's David again.

"Sarah? I'm coming down there if I don't see you walking this way in two minutes."

"I'm…leaving now, David. I promise."

I walk out of Dad's bedroom, closing the door behind me. I don't go back into my room, but I shut that door as well. As I descend the staircase, I notice the ominous haze has grown darker in color with the approaching dusk. It now looks like the cloud of dust a truck might leave behind when barreling down a gravel road, and I imagine that road, that truck. I try to see inside that plume of churning dirt, but it's impenetrable, like a solid wall of cement. There's no dark and hideous creature lurking within it, just a mass of secrets too scary to share with a little girl.

I step out the front door, and as I close it behind me, I feel a weakness in my legs. I walk forward a bit and stop, then continue, not turning around to look back. There's an ache in my chest. As it spreads into the deepest parts of my body, it carries with it the undeniable message—as much as I don't want to believe it—that I'll never see the inside of my house again.

~14~

At 7 o'clock, the alarm on Alex's cell phone goes off. The air in the small room is colder than normal. George turned off the central heating unit when he left on Sunday night, as he did every night, but because he hadn't been back since, the shop went without heat all day yesterday. Alex remains tucked inside his sleeping bag for a few minutes longer, partly because of the chilly air and partly because of the gnawing deep inside his stomach, like parasites trying to chew their way out. He didn't expect to wake up this morning without it, but he'd hoped it might not be so apparent.

He pulls his legs out from inside the warmth of the sleeping bag and hurries to the shower. He turns the nozzle as far to the right as it will go, then waits for the water to heat up before turning it back down to a bearable temperature. He washes his hair, his body. He drops his chin toward the ground and lets the water soak the back of his head and neck. The warmth moves across his shoulders and into his back, then over his butt and down the length of his legs. He imagines it's not water caressing his body, but a hundred small fingers, kneading and rubbing and touching his skin. He has an erection, but he doesn't let it go this time. He takes himself in his hands, and when he reaches climax, he pretends the parasites that chew at his insides are released from his body. When he opens his eyes, he sees the sticky whiteness disappear into the shower drain.

He dresses himself in jeans and a navy blue t-shirt, and then brushes his teeth. His right eye is black and blue, and his nose is swollen. There's also a small crack in his upper lip, just below the tip of his nose. He purposefully didn't use the frozen pack of peas last night. He even considered punching himself a few times in the left eye, for an even stronger effect, but he was too tired to do anything more than nibble on some turkey slices from the refrigerator.

He sits on the edge of the cot and reaches beneath it for the gun case. He removes the Glock, and then pushes the case back until it's pressed up against the far wall, making it invisible unless a person is down on his hands and knees, or unless the cot is removed altogether. He isn't sure why he did it. If someone really wants the case, it'll be found.

He takes a raspberry Pop Tart from the box George brought him last week, but when he opens the small pouch, the sweet sugary odor that escapes from it makes his stomach go sour. He puts the pouch back in the box and drops the box in the garbage can. He tucks the Glock into his jeans and pulls his windbreaker over his head. He'll need to keep the windbreaker on this morning. The t-shirt alone isn't enough—the outline of the gun can easily be seen by anybody walking toward him.

Alex walks through the gun shop one more time before exiting out the back door and into the alley. He locks the door and tucks the key into the front pocket of his jeans. The sky is gray with dark clouds, and puddles of brown water dot the gravel roadway. It rained last night, but he doesn't remember hearing it. The smell of damp earth is thick in the alley, but after walking a few blocks away from town and into the tree-lined street that leads to the high school, the muddy odor is replaced by the scent of lilacs and petunias and geraniums, and evergreen needles soaked in fresh rainwater.

As he continues walking, Alex keeps his eyes on the sidewalk and avoids stepping on the cracks. Cars drive by, coming and going, some with loud music blaring from stereos. Students mostly. He doesn't pay attention to them, not even when someone shouts from an open car window, "How's the nose, Mackey?" It isn't Joe Berger's voice, but a friend of his who was probably one of the first Joe bragged to.

When Alex finally reaches the middle school, he stops for a few minutes. Cars pull up, kids jump out. A group of girls stand near the front doors talking and giggling. At the northeast corner of the building, two boys are picking on a smaller one. The bigger of the boys is gripping the small kid's backpack, preventing him from moving forward.

"Let go!" the small kid barks.

"Make me," the bigger boy says.

The other boy takes the small kid's baseball hat from his head and holds it high up in the air.

"Give it back," the small kid says.

Alex has the urge to walk over to the group and press the nose of the gun to the back of the boy's head who's holding the hat. Instead, he watches the scene continue to unfold, frustration and anger burning inside of him as he thinks of his own humiliation at the hands of others. He turns and continues walking toward the high school. He enters the building through the south doors, knowing Sarah and her friends sometimes mingle near the staircase before the bell rings. It's still pretty early, though, and they're not there, which is exactly how Alex wants it.

According to the large digital clock hanging above the lockers in the senior hallway, it's 7:51. The first bell rings at 8:10. The second at 8:15. As long as David is in the senior cafeteria where he'd normally be at this time, Alex's plan should work accordingly. He's not concerned about Joe being absent today. He wouldn't miss the opportunity to showcase his artistic skills, so eloquently painted on Alex's face, to the entire senior class, in the cafeteria, the morning after he worked so hard.

Alex puts his backpack in his locker and walks into the cafeteria. Dustin is sitting at the end of the table where they meet just about every morning. He waves to Alex, and Alex returns the gesture, then walks up and sits across from him. David and the rest of the group are gathered near the wall of windows, right where Alex hoped they'd be. Sarah and Megan are sitting across from each other at the end of the table—Sarah's back is to Alex—and David, Jalen, Reggie and Randy are standing just to the left of the table. The only person missing is Emma, but it's not unusual for her to show up right before the first bell rings, if she shows up early at all. She's been late to economics at least once each week since the school year started. Mr. Grey even gave her the nickname Mostly Tardy Morgan.

"Did you hear me?" Dustin asks.

Alex turns to him. "Huh?"

"You've been out of it since yesterday, dude. What's with you?"

"What do you mean?"

Dustin frowns. "I don't know, man, but you're acting all strange. You didn't bother showing up last Saturday night after you decided to go to that stupid fair, which is just fucked up on its own, and all day yesterday you barely said one word. And why didn't you call me after Joe did that to your face?"

Alex shrugs. "It's no big deal. How'd you find out?"

"You're kidding, right? It doesn't take a genius to figure it out."

"Sorry."

"Look, Alex," Dustin says, "I know things are all messed up for you at home, but that's never stopped you from coming over and hanging out. It just seems like there's something else bothering you."

Alex turns to look at the digital clock hanging above the door to the boy's bathroom. It's 8:01. If Dustin doesn't shut-up, he's going to ruin the whole thing.

"See what I mean," Dustin says. "You're not listening to a fucking word I'm saying."

Alex lays his hands flat on the table. The parasitic gnawing has returned to the pit of his stomach. He can't let anything get in his way now. Not Dustin, not the pain in his gut. He has no friends here, only enemies. George knew that better than anyone. And George is the only person who's ever given a shit about him, and now he's dead, and all that's left is Dustin. Weak. Annoying. Sits and says nothing, does nothing Dustin.

Alex looks around the cafeteria. Joe Berger is standing across the room, surrounded by a group of his friends who are staring at Alex and laughing.

"Leave me alone, Dustin," Alex says without meeting his gaze.

Dustin stands up from the table. "Fuck you, Alex." He storms out of the cafeteria and disappears around the corner into the senior hallway.

Alex feels a sharp pain in his chest, like he's been stabbed in the heart with a dagger, but he closes his eyes and wills the tears away.

Get over it, Alex. You're stronger than this.

He rises from his seat. The digital clock says 8:04. Reggie and Jalen have moved away from David and Randy and are now seated at the table next to Sarah and Megan. Alex walks toward them, the blood pumping so loudly in his ears it drowns out the voices and laughter from the packed cafeteria. Halfway to the wall of windows, he turns and makes eye contact with Joe. He smiles and nods his head.

Fuck you, Joe.

Joe frowns, and as Alex turns back to David and Randy, he sees Joe moving toward him.

Perfect. Come on, asshole.

He's nearly to David now. Randy taps David on the shoulder and says something, then points to Alex. David turns toward him and smiles. He can't hear any voices at all now, just the whoosh of blood, the thumping of his heart, the chewing and biting and ripping of the parasites in his stomach. His eye and nose throb, his lip aches, his hands are on fire. Hot. Wet. Burning.

He keeps his eyes on David and thinks of George. The pain in his gut subsides a little. He wonders if George is watching. He hopes so. But then he stops. Sarah is stepping away from the table. She turns toward David. She's smiling.

Wait. Why is she here? If George is dead, why is she here? Why is she smiling?

It hadn't crossed Alex's mind until now.

"You're lookin' pretty hot with that shiner, Mackey." Joe is standing just a few inches away.

Alex drops his eyes to the floor. He feels the gun pressed against his belly.

"Leave him alone, Joe." It's Sarah's voice, like a child's, sweet and pure and gentle.

He looks up to meet her gaze, and when he does, the painful gnawing in the pit of his stomach creeps up into his chest and then into his throat. He can't breathe. He turns around to walk away. "I need…to go."

"Not so fast, punk," Joe snaps.

He grabs Alex's left arm and pulls him forward. Alex feels the gun jump, as though it's trying to free itself from his jeans. With his right hand, he reaches under his windbreaker and t-shirt and grips the Glock, then pulls the weapon out, one finger on the trigger, the rest squeezing the handle.

When Joe sees the gun, he lets go of Alex's arm, and Alex falls backwards, the gun slipping in his sweat-soaked hand. In his attempt to gain control of it, he squeezes the trigger. The sound is deafening—sharp and deep like a wild crack of thunder—and within seconds of it piercing the stuffy cafeteria, the room fills with screams. There is chaos, and then Alex is sitting on the floor. He sees legs first, running, then bodies falling as students push each other to the ground, and then more legs trampling the bodies that have fallen. The screaming escalates. There's yelling and crying... and blood. On the floor not far from his feet and moving toward him like a slow-running rivulet. The gun is lying next to him, not yet touched by the mass of traveling feet, as though it's his child, keeping close to him for protection from the stampede.

Alex doesn't see Joe Berger. He's gone, disappeared with so many others who've already run out the emergency doors. An ear-piercing siren erupts—long crescendo whistles, several seconds long, playing over and over and over again. It's the school's fire alarm.

The snake-like rivulet of blood reaches his shoe and wraps itself around his heel like spilled milk to the foot of a table's leg. He follows its path and sees David sitting on his knees, his hands covering his face. Megan is there too, also on her knees. Her mouth is open. Alex thinks she might be screaming, but he can't hear her over the fire alarm. Is it her blood? David's? Alex missed him. Missed his head or neck or heart.

But the blood isn't either of theirs. It's coming from the body they're hovering over, her jean-clad legs sticking out, but her upper body and face hidden from his view by David.

Oh, please. No.

David shifts from his knees onto his butt, turning outward as he moves, and when he does, Alex sees Sarah. Her shirt is soaked in blood. It's in her hair, on her face, covering her arms. Megan and David's clothes are also doused in blood, splattered across their shirts and jeans like a new-age painting. Megan is crying hysterically and rocking back and forth, her arms crossed over her chest. David's face is blank, empty, almost lifeless itself.

Alex can't breathe. He tucks his chin into his chest, his arms over his belly. He pulls his knees up. He's sick.

What have I done? Oh, George. George, I'm so sorry. It was an accident. It was an accident.

The fire alarm continues to cry its painful wails, screaming for somebody to come help. To Alex, it seems like hours have passed. Where are the police? Where is the ambulance? But it's only been minutes. The cafeteria has mostly cleared out, but a few teachers linger by the emergency doors. They've probably been instructed to remain outside until the gunman and his weapon have been removed. David and Megan won't leave. Nobody can make them leave.

The pain in Alex's stomach is gone, replaced by a harsh emptiness that rises up into his chest and swallows his heart like a deathly virus. It hurts, but not like the gnawing parasites. The pain is deeper, stronger. It moves through his entire body, infecting every muscle and bone, contaminating his blood. It's a dark and hollow pain, and he knows there's no escape from it.

He picks up the gun and turns toward David. Their eyes meet, but David doesn't see him. It's as though Alex doesn't exist, as though he's already dead. He looks at the Glock—thick and dark and real. It's warm to the touch, like his mother's fingers when she used to take his hand in hers and they'd walk home together, laughing and talking, sharing stories about school and work and life. They were good stories. Happy stories. Funny stories.

Alex raises the gun and presses the nose of it to his temple. When he pulls the trigger, the fire alarm stops screaming. The cafeteria disappears into an explosion of hot white light, and he's floating. Floating. And beneath him, far away, too far away now for Alex to see, police officers and firemen and paramedics descend upon the school.

~15~

The sound was deafening, like the M80 someone set off during the 4th of July parade in Kalispell a few years ago. Main Street was lined with people, smiling and waving, and then there was an explosion that caused everyone to pause for a brief second in silent wonder. One person probably screamed, and then moms were gathering up their kids and running while men were scrambling around trying to figure out who was responsible.

I see faces. I hear voices. There's a rush of movement all around me. And at first, I feel nothing except a wet heat spilling down my chest. I don't notice the blood until I look at the floor, and then I'm falling into it. When I open my eyes, I see the hazy whiteness of the ceiling in the cafeteria. David and Megan are sitting beside me, but they're not looking at me. I hear the wail of the school's fire alarm, and then another loud bang, far away from me, outside of the black that surrounds me. I slide my arm across the cold laminate flooring until my hand hits something. It's David's leg. He jumps. I don't see him anymore, but I feel his fingers on my face.

"Sarah," he says, his voice sounding far away, even though I know his mouth is now just inches from mine. "Talk to me, baby. Talk to me."

I want to, but I can't. My lips and tongue are burning hot one second and then ice cold the next. I hear my heart beating, but it's a slow, muffled sound like it's been wrapped in a wet towel. It speeds up for a minute, loud and strong as though it's trying to break free, but then it slows way down again, defeated by the heavy weight pressing against it. I feel the thumping in my chest, like fingers tapping on my rib cage. It doesn't hurt really, but it's a strange feeling, like something's trapped inside me trying to find a way out.

David's voice is nearly gone now, and I'm no longer in the cafeteria. I'm standing at the edge of Julie Allen's dock, staring into the water. It's as still as glass and crystal clear, the rocks at the bottom a rainbow of rich shades of blues and greens and purples. I'm not really here. I know that. I'm lying on the floor in a puddle of blood, my blood, spilling out of me and taking my life with it. And not just my life, but also that of the baby growing inside me. My baby. David's baby. The one the world didn't want to know, and now won't.

It's okay, though. I don't have to be afraid to make this decision anymore. It's been made for me. I saw the gun in Alex's hand. I know what happened, and I know where the weapon came from.

"...and I'm sorry for whatever happens now. I only hope you can forgive me someday..."

This isn't happening to me. I don't want to go away now. Not yet. *Oh, Daddy. Why?*

I'm in the backyard dribbling a soccer ball between my knees, small and far away. I hear Dad's voice, gentle like the wind, and then I'm racing down the mountain, snow and ice whipping through my hair and across my cheeks. I see Dad at the bottom of the hill, waving. I run to him, wrap my arms around his thick neck and squeeze.

When I move away, he's crying. He grips his chest and falls to his knees, and I place my hand on top of his head, but he can't feel my fingers. I step back and look around the living room, all of my artwork gone—the clock and the needlepoint framed in Popsicle sticks, the watercolor of a fruit bowl and the trinket basket. It's all gone, and I smell the stench of rotting bananas and spoiled milk.

I don't want to die.

I squeeze my eyes shut and try to reach for David in the blackness. Behind my lids, I see bleachers full of people. They're moving in slow motion, clapping and cheering and stomping their shoes against the metal slats beneath their feet. The sound should be unbearable, but I can't hear anything. I'm standing at the end of one long row, but nobody seems to notice me.

I look out at a football field where two teams are lined up opposite each other. One team wears yellow and blue, the other red and white. I'm standing at the edge of the field now, below the bleachers and close enough to the cheerleaders wearing yellow and blue that I can feel the rush of air from the unified movement of their pom poms. Like the people in the stands, the cheerleaders are moving in slow motion, but there's no sound at all, not even with the wind that's twisting my hair.

I walk onto the football field and toward the two teams. I don't hear the familiar words of the quarterback on the yellow and blue team shouting for the hike of the ball, but all of the players suddenly come alive, running and pushing and tackling one another. One of the blue and yellow players runs toward me. The quarterback throws him the ball. He catches it and turns, and as he runs in my direction, I see the familiar light brown of his eyes, the beautiful dark of his skin. I yell his name, but he runs past me and into the end zone. And then I hear the crowd, and I watch David's teammates surround him, and in the stands, I see Yvette and Clarence and Rayna, and a pretty blonde girl with green eyes waving a UCLA flag. But it's not me.

I open my eyes and look out across the lake at the Mission Mountains in the distance. It's a beautiful day. The sun is shining, the sky is the richest blue I've ever seen, and the water is a sheet of shiny green, shimmering beneath a magnificent burst of light like a million glittering diamonds. I sit at the edge of the dock, wrap my arms around my legs, and rest my head on my knees. And then I feel David's breath on my skin as he presses his lips to the back of my neck. He sits behind me and folds his arms across my body, embracing me as though he's afraid I might fall into the water. His body is warm.

We sit together for a long time, quiet. He's not really here with me, but I feel him. I smell him. I can taste him on my tongue as though his mouth is pressed to mine. But I'm scared to move because I know when I do, he'll be gone, and so will I, and everything that I am or was will also be gone. I'll be nothing but a memory, a photograph in a yearbook, a name beneath a remembrance plaque.

"I forgive you, Daddy," I say, and when I open my eyes, the light is bright and warm, and it sings to me like the birds in the trees.

~Epilogue~

The Kalispell Daily News

April 21, 2012

A Mystery Unravels in the Death of Two Kalispell High School Students

Eighteen-year-old Sarah Ann McKnight died last Tuesday morning at 8:07 from a single gunshot wound to the neck. Her memorial service on Saturday was attended by over 600 residents of the Kalispell and surrounding communities, including nearly every member of Kalispell High School's student body, faculty and staff; employees from the Big Mountain Ski Resort in Whitefish; and many others who didn't personally know her, but who were moved by her story.

According to local authorities, Ms. McKnight's death was considered an accident. Three minutes after she was hit, Alex Eugene Mackey (also 18) took his own life with the same Glock 19. The weapon came from McKnight Company, a gun shop on Main Street owned by George McKnight, Ms. McKnight's father. Mackey had been working for Mr. McKnight for two years. It was initially believed Mackey's possession of the gun was made possible because of the destruction of a primary display case at the front of the shop where the weapon had been stored. Later reports indicate, however, that Mr. McKnight had not only given the gun to Mackey, but had also showed him how to use it on a recent visit to First Stop Firing Range on Highway 2 outside of Kalispell.

The whereabouts of George McKnight remained a mystery until last Friday morning, three days after the accident, when he walked into the Royal Mounted Canadian Police Station in Fernie, British Columbia—120 miles north of Kalispell—and turned himself in. He'd found out about his daughter's death

over the radio. He carried with him two different passports— one of George Marshall McKnight and the other of John Allen Lacey. He also carried his Montana State driver's license and an additional driver's license from the state of Alabama, also with the name John Allen Lacey.

In a raid of McKnight Company, it was discovered that George McKnight had been running, for almost two decades, an underground weapons operation, supplying guns and ammunition to a number of different Ku Klux Klan chapters in Alabama and Mississippi. This discovery has led to the arrests of several KKK members for their involvement in a handful of previously unsolved murder cases in both states.

Testimony from George McKnight revealed his hope that Alex Mackey would use the Glock 19 on David Brooks, an 18-year-old African-American student at Kalispell High School. Brooks is an avid student and athlete. He was recently offered a full-ride football scholarship to the University of California in Los Angeles. McKnight had been "mentally manipulating" Mackey because of a suspicion that his only daughter was dating Brooks. This suspicion was confirmed on the Saturday night before the shooting. Ms. McKnight and Brooks had plans to move to California in August. She was also enrolled at UCLA. At the time of her death, she was ten weeks pregnant.

George McKnight expected Mackey to be arrested, leading police to the gun shop and underground operations. The John Allen Lacey passport and driver's license had been in his possession for years in case any of the guns supplied to the KKK were ever traced back to him. Kalispell's close proximity to the Canadian border had been just one of several reasons why McKnight chose to move there.

Not much is known about George McKnight's past. Both of his parents passed away by the time he turned 18. He'd lived temporarily with friends, had worked a few odd jobs in Alabama (including 20+ years for a man named Brad Placid who was later arrested for gun-trafficking), and later moved to Kalispell with his then 2-month-old daughter. Although responsible for a number of heinous crimes due to his 17 years of supplying weapons to the KKK, McKnight has never been arrested himself, and he's never used a gun on anything other than paper targets on shooting ranges.

Like McKnight, very little is known about Alex Mackey. He was a bright student, but he was considered a loner. His friend, Dustin Binger, claimed to know nothing about the plan, although he did comment that Alex had been acting "strange" in the days leading up to the shooting. Alex's parents—Chuck and Mary Mackey—would not comment on their son. An anonymous source at Kalispell Memorial Hospital said Mary Mackey had been admitted a number of times in a span of five years for lacerations and bruises, as well as broken bones in her hands. This source believed Mrs. Mackey's injuries were a result of domestic violence, but no charges have ever been filed against Chuck Mackey.

George McKnight is being held without bail and is currently under suicide watch. Kalispell residents closest to George and Sarah McKnight expressed shock and sadness. Marge Adams, a long-time friend of George's, was "deeply saddened by Sarah's death and equally outraged by George's deceit".

"I've known George for almost 20 years," Adams said. "He pulled the wool right over my eyes, over a lot people's eyes in this town. I'm still not sure I believe it."

CPSIA information can be obtained at www.ICGtesting.com
Printed in the USA
LVOW12s1928281213

367247LV00021B/1789/P